Quickies – 8
A Black Lace erotic short-story collection

Quickies – 8
A Black Lace erotic short-story collection

BLACKLACE

Black Lace books contain sexual fantasies.
In real life, always practise safe sex.

This edition published in 2007 by
Black Lace
Thames Wharf Studios
Rainville Road
London W6 9HA

Typeset by SetSystems Limited, Saffron Walden, Essex

Printed in the UK by CPI Bookmarque, Croydon, CR0 4TD

ISBN 978 0 352 34137 1

Derailed Cal Jago

We had been waiting inside the tunnel for almost ten minutes. The carriage was heaving as usual – it was rush hour after all – and people were being their usual tetchy selves when it came to rail disruption. The air was full of tuts and sighs and commuters dramatically checked their watches or stood mute, frowning, with the odd 'can you believe it?' eye roll thrown in for good measure. The situation wasn't helped by the heat. A young man dressed casually in jeans and a T-shirt, who looked far too sleepy to be setting out for the day, pressed his right cheek against the door in an attempt to find some coolness. He had been standing like that, stooped and heavy lidded, for the past five stops.

I stood sideways on to the set of doors opposite Sleepy, my back against the glass separating me from the seated passengers, my briefcase held neatly in front of my knees. Just in front of me a woman with a rucksack bearing the slogan 'Designers are Crazy Bastards' was looking from the crumpled tube map in her hand to the map on the wall above the door and back again. To my right, a middle-aged man frowned into a book whose title claimed to be able to teach him Italian in seven days. I was sceptical.

The person who interested me most, however, was leaning against the doors to my left. Thick dark hair emphasised the blueness of his eyes and full lips pouted from a shadow of stubble. He held a rolled-up copy of *Q* magazine but clearly wasn't interested in it as he hadn't looked at it all the time he'd been on the train. Out of the corner of my eye I noticed him smile as the driver made a garbled announcement, indecipherable due to persistent crackling.

And then the lights went out.

Well, that really pissed them all off. As I listened to people complain and try to outdo each other by being more in a rush than everyone else – because their life was busier than anyone else's – I simply smiled and saw the situation for what it was: an opportunity.

The heat seemed to swell the moment we were plunged into darkness. An uneasy hush fell upon the carriage as the lights failed to immediately come back on as expected. I stood perfectly still for a few seconds as anticipation shot through my body like an electric force. My eyes gradually became accustomed to the lack of light and I began to make out the silhouettes of my fellow commuters. Bizarrely, Crazy Bastard still appeared to be hunched over her map, holding the paper up to her eyes in a desperate attempt to activate her see-in-the-dark super powers.

I cleared my throat and slowly reached down and placed my briefcase on the floor. As I straightened up, I turned my body so that I stood directly in front of Q. My skin tingled. In the eerily silent carriage the roar of my blood rushing in my ears was deafening. Then, ever so slowly, I took a small step backwards with my left foot and failed to suppress a sigh, which escaped from my lips and hung in the silent blackness, as my arse made contact with Q's thigh.

I shifted my weight from one foot to the other, the movement positioning my buttocks over his groin. I smiled. I knew he was smiling too; I could feel it on the back of my neck. I hovered there for a few seconds relishing the anticipation of the moment. Then, keeping the rest of my body absolutely still, I pushed my arse out slightly and finally made the contact with him that I craved. I remained still allowing him to feel the pressure of me against him. Then I gently swung my hips from side to side, exhilarated by the sensation of his excitement pushing against me. As I leant back into him more firmly every nerve ending in my body buzzed. This was going to be a good one, I could feel it.

Perfect timing then for the lights to flash back on and the train to lurch to life. Thrown off balance I reached up to grab the overhead handrail and in that split second the contact between his body and mine was lost. Feeling suddenly light headed, I gripped the handrail tighter as we approached the next station. I quickly looked around to see any obvious signs of my behaviour having been spotted. Crazy Bastard was now tracing a route along her map with her finger and Sleepy's eyes remained half shut. Elsewhere, the return of light had put reading and make-up application back on the agenda. No one appeared to have noticed mine and Q's small but significant indiscretion. As we roared to a stop at the next station, my tight chest and damp knickers and the presence of Q again nudging against my arse made it clear what I absolutely needed to do. As the doors whooshed open, I scooped up my briefcase, spun on my heels and flung myself on to the crowded platform.

I was swept along for a few frantic seconds, caught up in the wildebeest-esque herd of commuters until, at the mouth to the exit, the mass bottlenecked causing a jam. We stood packed together, all trying to pigeon-step our way forwards. Anxiety bubbled in my chest as I waited. I darted into a small gap and pushed my way up the steps, no doubt annoying everyone around me. But I had to get out. I had to breathe.

Once outside, I took a deep breath, filling my lungs with exhaust fumes and passing cigarette smoke and taking comfort in the roar of traffic. I looked at my watch and sighed as I began the long walk to the office.

My underground – and, for that matter, overground – train adventures could fill a book. Illicit liaisons with strangers in packed public places – what could be more delicious? There are times when the only thing that's got me through my working day is knowing that I'll soon be stepping into a new carriage, a new playground. Trains are my thing. I have lost count of the number of men and women I have teased, groped and generally been filthy with around the national rail network.

And yet, here I am having alighted four stops too soon about to walk the rest of the way to the office. So why have I just walked out on a great hit? Have I had a bad experience? Did I target the wrong person? Was I caught on camera and forcibly removed from a train and banned forever by Transport for London? No. Basically, I'm just trying to amend my ways. For the past three months I've been officially sort of 'seeing someone' and I figured that, early days or not, curbing my public-transport groping ways is probably the least I can do. But my God it's a struggle.

Dan and I met at a work thing. He had coveted the best art director award at a magazine do and so, when I found myself standing next him at the bar later, I offered him my congratulations. We already knew each other vaguely – same publishing house, different magazines – but our relationship up until that point had barely stretched beyond 'good mornings' and the odd eye roll in mundane meetings. But something must have happened that night as we celebrated with canapés and strawberry bellinis because a few days later, when he appeared in my office with offerings of a mocha and a muffin and asked me if I fancied going for dinner sometime, I said yes. I think he may have caught me off guard. Nevertheless, dinner the following evening had been a triumph and what followed that night back at my place, even more so.

A few months later all was going surprisingly well. And that made me slightly nervous. Not that Dan and I were serious. It was all just very light and fun and casual. And sexual. It's just that I'm very good at being single. I like to do my own thing, play by my rules and come whenever I like with whomever I like. And that's why I had almost gone into meltdown about Brighton.

'I've got to go to that conference next weekend,' he had told me through a mouthful of linguine one night.

I pulled a face. 'Lucky you. The agenda looks truly scintillating.'

'You're not going then?'

'Nope.' I had topped up our glasses with Shiraz and smiled. 'Budget cuts. They've almost halved the number of delegates and managing editors have been given the chop.' I took a gulp of wine. 'Damn shame. At least you'll be by the sea.'

'Come with me,' he'd said.

I had laughed. 'Are you asking me or telling me?'

He'd smiled. 'I'm asking you. But of course you have to say yes.'

I'd fallen suddenly serious. 'I'm not invited, remember?'

'I'm inviting you – as my guest in the hotel room. You can shop your way around the Lanes during the day, then we can do something in the evening. We could even make a weekend of it.'

I'd frowned. 'A weekend away?' I'd asked. 'Together?'

'Christ, Kate. I'm not asking you to marry me! I just want to take you to a hotel for a couple of days so we can quaff champagne and fuck each other senseless.'

Well, when he put it like that, nothing about the suggestion seemed to contravene any of my relationship-phobic sensibilities. So Brighton was on.

By the time I made it to my office I was almost an hour late and had already missed the start of a meeting. Natalie, my assistant, raised an eyebrow as I rushed in.

'Trains,' I said simply by way of explanation and headed for the meeting room. And despite my good intentions, flashbacks to Q and the possibilities of the journey home were already all I could think of.

* * *

The week passed quickly. Work was hectic and, besides meetings, I felt that I barely saw or spoke to anyone. At home on the Thursday evening I put on a CD and sank into my favourite chair, exhausted after another manic day during which I felt I had hardly achieved anything important due to the hours spent responding to constant emails. I was in the middle of convincing myself to never turn my computer on again when my front door buzzed and there was Dan.

'Brighton's tomorrow, isn't it?' I said rather abruptly.

He laughed. 'Yes. But it's not actually a crime to see each other on consecutive days.'

I wondered if perhaps it should be, but let him in all the same.

You know how you sometimes have evenings where you didn't set out to want to do anything or see anyone or make any effort at all and then before you know it something happens and you're having a good time? Or how you think to yourself, a quiet evening in, an early night, perhaps one glass of wine but that's it. And then you find yourself whooping and shrieking and laughing into the early hours convinced that you'll never come down for long enough to ever be able to sleep again? Well, that's how it came to be that Dan and I were both sitting on the floor of my lounge, smashed on an ancient bottle of tequila that Dan had found in my kitchen and sharing intimate thoughts and anecdotes with each other at four in the morning.

Through the highbrow medium of drinking games, I had learnt all sorts of personal details about Dan and had made a fair few revelations myself. The tequila, my tiredness, the intimacy and the varied sexual confessions had a potent effect on me; before I knew that I was even considering saying it, I heard myself boldly confess my most secret hobby.

'So I've touched all these men,' I was saying. 'And quite a few women. And I touch them until they lose all control and all they can think about is coming. People who would never think they were capable of such behaviour. But they do it for me, surrounded by all those people, because suddenly the only thing that matters to them is that I don't take my hand away.'

It was the first time I had ever confessed to it and once I started I couldn't stop. On and on I went, explaining how it felt, trying so hard to convey the absolute thrill of it. I was wet just talking about it. But it was a while before I realised that Dan had been silent for some minutes.

'What a dark horse you are,' he said when he finally spoke. He gave me a sideways look. 'Who'd have thought it, eh?'

'Have I shocked you?' I giggled and leant towards him to kiss him. I really wanted him then. I really wanted us to go to bed.

'A bit,' he said seriously as my mouth was just a fraction from his.

I hovered where I was for a moment before moving to sit back down again. I frowned. 'I don't even know why I just told you that,' I said lightly. 'It's really not a big deal.' But the awkward silence between us told me it was too late.

Dan cleared his throat and slowly stood up. 'I'd better get going or I won't be in any fit state tomorrow.'

'You can stay if you like?' I said casually. 'It's late.'

He shook his head. 'No, I need to get home tonight.' He kissed me lightly on the top of my head. 'See you tomorrow.'

'Six o'clock at Victoria?'

He looked at me blankly for a moment.

'Brighton?'

He smiled and nodded and then he was gone.

Standing by the coffee cart at Victoria station the following evening could have been very *Brief Encounter* but, as it happened, it wasn't. Dan was nowhere to be seen. I tried to look nonchalant as I sipped my cappuccino and I attempted to shake the feeling that I must have looked like I'd been stood up. Or perhaps, the feeling that I really couldn't shake was that, actually, I probably had been stood up.

I hadn't heard from Dan since my revelation the previous evening and the more I thought about it, the more cross I was with myself for blabbing and the more clearly I recalled the serious expression on his face. Part of me believed that it was his problem if he wasn't able to deal with a small sexual peccadillo but I also felt embarrassed by my clumsy confession.

I still felt twitchy. Even if I was being paranoid and Dan was on his way he was cutting it fine. There were five minutes to go before departure.

My phone beeped signalling a new text.

'Held up at work. You've got your ticket anyway so might as well just meet you at the hotel. Dan.'

I reread the message. It hardly sounded enthusiastic. Was this my cue to go home? Was its formal tone Dan's way of telling me not to bother? Or was I simply misinterpreting his message because I already felt on edge?

'For fuck's sake,' I muttered and then I tossed my empty coffee cup into the nearby litter bin and strode across the concourse towards my platform.

I glanced at my ticket; typically, my seat was in the farthest carriage. I hopped on board as lithely as one can when carrying a suitcase and wearing high heels. As the door was slammed shut behind me I stood wedged between it and the back of the man who had got on just before me. In front of him stood a queue of people, each shuffling forwards on a mission to find a seat. I gripped my ticket impatiently and sighed as I resigned myself to the fact that there was no point in trying to barge through to my seat. I would just have to wait.

On the opposite side of the vestibule area a man had already taken his chances, opting out of the shuffle simply to secure a decent standing space. He pressed himself back against the door behind him to allow the shufflers to move past him more easily. As the crowds began to disperse and I had progressed to standing in front of him, it struck me how perfect he looked. How absolutely my type. Approaching forty, he was dressed in a plain dark suit – Armani, I noticed, from the label inside the jacket, which was revealed when he removed it and slung it over one arm. His fairish hair was greying slightly and he had some fine lines around his pale-blue eyes. He looked a little quiet. Shy perhaps. Like I said: perfect. Even shy people need to let themselves go sometimes and when they do it's nice to be around to witness it.

As commuters began to move along the carriage I

watched Armani gradually relax as more space opened up around him and I suddenly felt an over-whelming sense of longing. Apart from short instances of surreptitious train friction, I had been a very well-behaved girl over the past few months. No teasing, no grinding, no touching. And, oh, how I'd missed it. And now Dan was being an arse, my libido had gone into overdrive and here I was standing near the perfect Armani. Could I really be blamed if I were to seize this opportunity? Wouldn't it serve Dan right? And, more to the point, wouldn't it feel good to regain a sense of my old single self again?

Ahead of me a woman with four children and twice as many Hamleys bags was battling to get all her party along the aisle and safely into her reserved seats in the next carriage. She blocked the space entirely as she struggled. As I stood, lust momen-tarily gave way to irritation. I was irritated by the harassed mother for travelling with her brood during rush hour. I was irritated by her whiny children who continued to grizzle despite clearly having been bought half the contents of the world's most famous toy shop. I was irritated by my fellow commuters who did nothing to help her but simply exacerbated the crush by puffing their chests out and huffing loudly. I was irritated by the presence of Armani and the niggling thought that even though I wanted him I really shouldn't do anything about it although I tingled to my very core. But, of course, no prizes for guessing who I was most irritated with at that moment in time.

It was very appropriate, therefore, that on that thought the object of my fury came into view. The woman had managed to seat herself, the children grim and the numerous bags, so the crowd began to disperse. As I moved through the carriage and the crowd thinned as people found seats, my view cleared. And that is when I saw Dan sitting in his reserved seat reading a copy of *The Times*. I stopped suddenly and stared at him, amazed.

What the fuck was he playing at? He leaves me standing on my own looking like a social reject then annoys me with a grumpy text and all the time he was sitting on the train reading the paper? I frowned as I contemplated what to do. I was furious but I suppose it was petulant to make a point of standing all the way to Brighton on my own. And even if I did do that, what would things be like when we got there? Pissed off or not, I didn't want a weekend of awkward silences.

I sighed and started to move forwards but as I walked towards him a woman approached him and asked if the seat beside him was free. He looked up from his newspaper and smiled. Then, unbelievably, I noticed him glance fleetingly at me before telling her that it was indeed free as his travelling companion had missed the train. I stopped abruptly and stood still, incredulous. As the woman collapsed thankfully into the seat – *my* seat –Dan looked at me with a sly grin and an arched eyebrow before returning to his newspaper.

Shocked, I decided the best course of action was to retreat and gather my thoughts. Dan continued to stare at his newspaper but I could tell he wasn't reading anything on the page. I backed up until I was in the vestibule area again. Armani was now alone in the space. He looked up as I rejoined him.

'It's packed down there,' I said unnecessarily.

He smiled.

I snuck a peek at Dan as the door separating the vestibule from the carriage closed. Irritation had given way to curiosity now. I frowned slightly as I stared at him through the glass and tried to work out what he was up to. This was obviously a game. But quite what game we were playing I wasn't sure.

Armani had opened a book and begun to read. I was struck again by how attractive he was. There was something intense about him that I was drawn to; I liked the concentration on his face as he read. He was stockier than I had initially thought. He had a thick neck and strong forearms but I noticed that the hands which held his book steady were soft, his fingers on the book's spine, long and slim with perfectly smooth square fingernails.

A small train judder was required, I decided. A sudden lurch or a particularly bumpy stretch of track; all these factors that make a journey more uncomfortable for other passengers were things that I positively welcomed. After all, a girl has to reach out to steady herself if she feels herself falling. So I willed the train to jolt with all my might. And that's when a man with shoulders far too broad for public transport strolled through the door, forcing me closer to Armani in order to save myself from getting my ears knocked off. He lumbered through our space, pausing for a few moments to unwrap a sandwich. As he battled with the packaging, I made an effort to look terribly helpful and leant closer towards Armani to give Shoulders and his BLT more room to manoeuvre.

I smiled apologetically at Armani. 'Sorry,' I whispered as my chest made contact with his.

I was sure he blushed slightly as he smiled back. 'No problem.'

And then I slid my thigh between his legs.

Armani cleared his throat and shifted his weight slightly. I knew that the redness in his cheeks would have deepened but I didn't check to see. And I suspect that if I had looked at his face he would not have met my gaze. So instead I look at Shoulders who had accessed the sandwich but continued to look around in front of him, bemused.

'Here,' I said and reached across a little way and pressed the button to open the door.

He grinned and shook his head. 'Sorry. Thought it was automatic. Thanks.'

I increased the pressure of my thigh against Armani's crotch. Something was definitely stirring. 'You're welcome,' I said lightly.

As Shoulders disappeared through the door leaving Armani and I alone again, I did not move immediately. When I did finally, slowly, turn around, I saw Dan through the glass looking at me, his newspaper neatly folded in half on the table in front of him. He winked mischievously and, when I casually edged backwards so that my heels kissed Armani's toes, and his hardening cock grazed my arse, I knew that the game had begun. I just really hoped no one was planning on going to the buffet car any time soon.

I rocked against Armani firmly but slowly, resisting the temptation to grind like a harlot. My desperate desire to just grab him and fuck him there and then shocked me. But the reality was that playing in this sort of public situation you had to be as discreet as you could force yourself to be. Although the pair of us were alone for now, we were only separated from the crowds by a couple of sliding glass doors. The thought of that alone made me squirm in delight. But it was also a reminder that something a little more subtle than a full-on fuck in a vestibule was required.

I moved my hips slowly but rhythmically, keeping the pressure against him constant. His left hand moved to rest on the back of my thigh, the touch so hesitant, so gentle that it was barely perceptible. But I felt it like a flame burning through my skin. And feeling it confirmed that the games had commenced. The confirmation signal, whether it was a moan, a touch or a stonking great erection straining against my arse, was always a relief. Even if you are totally convinced that you've picked well – and that kind of complete conviction is rare – only when you've felt or heard or seen undisputable proof can you totally relax and really begin to enjoy the encounter.

His breathing became heavier as I increased the friction. As I moved, constantly aware of him pushing against my flesh, I imagined how he would look if I stepped away from him now and turned to face him. I pictured his face – flushed skin, muscles tight – and, turning my attention lower, I imagined the impressive bulge in his trousers begging for release. Sometimes I abandoned them then, that image of utter desire and complete helplessness frozen in my memory as I left them in the carriage and lost myself in the crowd on the platform. But this time I was sure I wasn't going anywhere prematurely.

Armani's hand disappeared for a moment before reappearing on the back of my thigh, this time underneath my skirt. I held my breath as his hand rode a little higher, his touch still butterfly light. His fingers fluttered around the tops of my stockings. He skimmed the lace and pressed himself against my buttocks more forcefully. I did like a man who appreciated expensive hosiery. He felt harder all of a sudden as I felt his ridge pressing against the cleft of my arse.

I leant forwards a little, then reached back and ran the palm of my hand across the front of his trousers. A blast of hot breath prickled the back of my neck as I couldn't resist any longer and squeezed along his length. And that's when Dan stood up.

I continued to touch Armani as Dan edged out of his seat and began to move his way along the carriage, heading towards us. He gripped his newspaper tightly in his hand, the crossword page flapping open in front of him as he walked. He stared at me hard and I struggled not to squirm as Armani's fingers pressed more insistently into my flesh. Excitement caught in my chest as I wondered whether I had gone too far. Dan's expression was unreadable as he came closer but he walked with purpose, his gaze never leaving mine. I probably should have played it safe and stopped doing what I was doing. Stroking a stranger's cock when the man you're sort of seeing is approaching is probably, on the whole, unwise. But I couldn't stop myself. I couldn't let him go. I had waited months for this and the knowledge that Dan knew what I was doing and knew that he had been watching turned me on even more.

Dan hesitated just as he arrived at the other side of the door and that's when he let his newspaper fall to his side and I saw that I didn't need to worry about having gone too far. It was very clear that he had enjoyed the show. Only then did I realise that Armani obviously had no idea that Dan was there and that we could be seen. I assumed that Armani had his eyes shut. Obviously, he was not used to playing in public. Closing one's eyes in such a situation was potentially dangerous, as he was about to find out.

As the door whooshed open, Armani's body froze in an instant – apart from his hand which rocketed out from under my skirt and then rested limply at his side. Dan moved into our space and then stopped. My right hand still held Armani's cock but I had become still too. Dan did not look at either of us at all, but straightened his newspaper up and then folded it and turned it over so that he was looking at the top half of the back page. Sport. Not Dan's thing at all but then I didn't believe for one second that he was reading it. I realised that, standing behind me, Armani would not have been able to see Dan's obvious arousal. As far as he was concerned, this was a stranger who had walked in on our indiscretion – whether he had seen everything or not he wasn't sure – so probably the best thing to do in his mind was to shrink into the background. I had other plans though. I couldn't let Armani be too mortified or scared. More to the point, I couldn't have that cock of his go to waste.

So I slowly reached back and touched him again, my gaze never once leaving Dan who I am sure, out of the corner of his eye, could see that play had resumed. I couldn't help but breathe a small sigh of relief when I gripped Armani again and found he was still hard. His entire body was tense, however, so the possibility of him losing his nerve and taking flight was still very real. We had to play this absolutely right or we would lose him.

I continued to squeeze along his length, gently but firmly. I kept my body movement minimal so that Armani could see that I was still being discreet but still his body felt tense behind me. Gripping him firmly, I began to rub him through his trousers, strokes as long and smooth as I could get them through the material and from the difficult angle I was working from. Then I worked my hand lower and reached back between his legs. He felt heavy in my hand, his balls cupped in my palm. I squeezed them before returning to stroke his shaft again. Bingo. Despite his severe reservations he was relaxing. His body wanted this as much as mine did.

I noticed Dan quickly glance around checking that no one was coming through either door. He took a couple of steps closer towards us and then, as he looked down at the sports page again, he pushed his right hand up the front of my skirt and slid his fingers over my underwear. Taken by surprise, I barely stifled a moan. I bit down on my bottom lip, painfully aware of how wet the material was on his fingertips. I continued to watch his face as he continued to stare at the newspaper. He was good; an expression of pure concentration, apparently focused on the sports report, remained on his face while his fingers roamed over my underwear, lingering maddeningly but never staying in one place for quite long enough. Divine frustration. I wondered whether Armani's eyes were open now and, if so, whether he could see where Dan's hand was. Did he know that he was part of our game? Or was he blissfully ignorant to everything around him because all he could focus on was whether he was going to come in his trousers?

Dan's fingers began to rub rhythmically back and forth right where I needed it most. I opened my eyes wide in alarm to try to tell him that it was too much, that I wouldn't last another minute if he did that, but he still wasn't looking at me. I concentrated on trying to make the scenario last but Dan had his own way of moving the action forwards.

'Pull her knickers down,' he said quietly, all the while looking somewhere to the side of us into the middle distance.

It was the most I could do not to come right there and then the moment I heard those words.

Armani was silent and still. I wondered whether he had heard Dan's instruction and I knew that Dan was holding his breath in anticipation, just as I was. Then both Armani's hands were holding my arse, gently kneading the flesh for a few seconds, before he hooked his fingers under my knickers and eased them over my buttocks and hips so that they came to rest halfway down my thighs. Without a moment's hesitation, Dan's fingers were inside me, filling my wetness, pushing himself deep.

I vaguely heard Armani murmur something close to my ear and then his hands were back on me, gliding over my stockings, caressing my arse, squeezing the hot flesh. And then I felt fuller still as another finger pushed inside me from behind. Together, Dan and Armani found a synchronicity that blew my mind.

I pushed myself back on Armani's fingers forcing

him deeper and imagined each man's fingers touching the other's inside me, sliding through my wetness and over each other's skin as they fucked me. And that naturally led me to imagining the pair of them fucking me for real like this, their hard cocks rubbing against each other inside me. I bit my lower lip hard as Dan's thumb flicked across my clitoris, his fingers still buried deep. He held his thumb across the swelling, rocking the tip of his thumb firmly, causing exquisite stimulation.

Armani was breathing hard behind me. As I tried to hang on for just a little while longer I felt him nudge me away slightly. His fingers remained inside me but I felt his other hand move behind my arse. The movement was followed by the barely audible yet unmistakable sound of a zip unfastening. Armani's hand knocked against my arse as he worked himself to further excitement. I imagined him pulling hard, his face taut with tension, his cock ready to explode. His speed increased and the contact of his fist against my buttock became more forceful and I looked at Dan just as he withdrew his fingers from inside me and pinched my clitoris hard. A sharp spasm of pleasure raged between my thighs and I came with such intensity that I'm sure I would have fallen down had the two men not been standing either side of me. And after a few more sporadic movements, Armani caught his breath and then became suddenly still before his body relaxed behind me.

Dan, flushed and still hard, stepped to the other side of the vestibule and breathed deeply. Armani cleared his throat and straightened his clothes. Rather touchingly, he rearranged my clothes too. I wasn't used to this post-fumble awkwardness – I never hung around that long.

The silence was broken by the train manager announcing our imminent arrival at the next station. Perfect timing. A couple of minutes sooner and we'd have had a stream of people traipsing through our little display. And perfect timing also because, when we came to a halt and a woman on the platform opened the door, my suitcase was conveniently beside me on the floor whereas Dan's was right the other end of the carriage.

'Excuse me,' I said in my sweetest voice and I picked up my luggage, pushed past an astounded Dan and stepped off the train.

I couldn't help but grin as I marched along the platform. For a moment I half expected Dan to suddenly appear beside me, panting after running to catch me up. But I knew I had been too fast for him to have realised what was happening, sped to the other end of the carriage, located his luggage and got himself off the train. I knew I had won.

I left the station and headed for the taxi rank. A taxi fare for the remainder of the journey wouldn't be cheap but seeing Dan's shocked expression had been worth it. I wondered what would be going through his mind now, stuck in the vestibule with Armani, but I didn't have the heart to be too cruel to the man who had done his utmost to accommodate my favourite kink. As I slid into the back of a cab and gave the driver the name of the Brighton hotel I sent Dan a text: 'Hope you didn't mind me getting off?'

His reply came through in seconds. 'Not at all . . . so long as I'm next.'

I relaxed into my seat and smiled. I could hardly wait.

Cal Jago's short stories have been featured in numerous Wicked Words collections.

The Silk Seller Maria Lloyd

Newly arrived in London, I discover that I am something of a voyeur.

I live in a Georgian house on a neat little square behind Oxford Street. The area is a quiet cul-de-sac, a no man's land between the rag trade, Soho, college buildings, and the exclusive medical clinics of Harley Street. Opposite my house, across the tiny square, is a discreet shop front – a Georgian Bay window filled with a peacock fan of beautifully coloured diaphanous fabric. There is a discreet brass plaque next to the shop's heavy, black-fronted door. It is inscribed simply, *R Sebastian, Purveyor of Silks*.

At night, the shop-front window is softly illuminated and the coloured fabrics – rich ambers, delicate mauves, crimsons and golds – all glow hyper real, a beacon that draws the eye away from the dark-railed gardens at the centre of the square.

In the morning, on my way to work, I often pause to admire the silks more closely. Sometimes the morning sun catches their hues through the shop window and makes them shine like liquid gemstones.

I watch with interest as the silk-shop customers arrive or depart. It seems business is mostly wholesale, but occasionally a rich private client deals with Mr R Sebastian direct.

A mother and daughter arrive by limousine,

dressed in beautiful saris, and seem destined to discuss a bridal outfit of vermillion and gold. A woman in dark glasses, perhaps an actress incognito, departs carrying a sample of swatches. She is still flicking through them when she steps into her cab. The most intriguing customer so far is a man in a sober business suit who arrives carrying a hold-all near the end of the working day – yet the only person to depart an hour later is a suspiciously tall woman, clad in a red silk dress, knee-high boots and ... clutching a hold-all.

People have a right to their private indulgences, their harmless vices, and I feel a little guilty becoming so familiar with the secrets of the silk trade across the way. But still I sit on the window seat of my little lounge, nursing a cup of coffee or forking up take-away noodles, watching the haven of exotica provided by R Sebastian, purveyor of silks.

I grow fond of Mr Sebastian, who regularly, with old-world chivalry, accompanies clients to their waiting cabs on the corner of the square. He is tall and elegant in the masculine sense. He is almost Mongolian in his looks, having dark wavy hair, high cheekbones, heavy eyelids, and skin like polished walnut. He has large dark eyes that dance with brandy and green-gold lights as he smiles and shakes hands with his customers. He wears tailored linen suits, always with immaculate silk shirts and ties.

He is a dedicated man. I watch him working late into the evening in a small office above the shop, dealing with outstanding paperwork and queries on the internet. He even lives above his business, in a neat bachelor flat on the top floor.

I like watching him, in the evenings, in his tasteful office. It is decorated a warm terracotta with silk prints hung in frames around the room. He works at a large desk, with an old-fashioned, green shaded lamp to supplement the glow from his laptop screen as the light dims. He looks stern yet serene in concentration.

Sometimes clients are invited into his office to conclude special orders, and they sit positioned to one side of his desk upon a stylish Mackintosh chair, with its distinctive high-backed lattice design. While he is talking to such clients he sometimes moves forwards to adjust the window blinds, which intrigues me, as I then cannot see what is going on and it drives me mad.

Sometimes, in the very early morning, Mr Sebastian goes jogging in shorts and vest, displaying tightly honed muscles. Occasionally, late at night, before he draws his bedroom curtains, I notice a light on in his flat above the office. I often make myself a mug of hot chocolate before going to bed and, if I angle my window seat correctly, I can see his handsome torso, the wide shoulders and the strong chest with its fuzz of dark hair. I am pretty certain he sleeps in silk pyjamas, or naked against silk sheets.

Wouldn't you, if you were a purveyor of silks?

One lazy Saturday afternoon, fresh from a late shower and wrapped in my kimono, I sit at my window seat with a glass of orange juice and watch Mr Sebastian as he welcomes another client. The sun briefly dazzles my eyes, and I swear that Mr Sebastian looks directly up at me. Has the light illuminated me? My pulse races as I guiltily return his half-smile, just in case, even while I retreat into shadow.

I have been so entranced with my clear view of his office and bedroom that it never occurred to me he may have watched me also, these summer mornings and evenings as I travel naked or in my kimono about my front room.

I know I should move away entirely. But my little game of voyeurism has become far too addictive. Still I sit and sip my juice and watch in the hopes of another glimpse of my neighbour.

I do not expect what happens next.

His office door opens, and he walks inside with his client. I shift in my seat until I can see them both, and the whole room, clearly illuminated by the slanting afternoon light.

She is a willowy blonde wearing an expensive tailored suit and spiky boots. He is very solicitous of her, seating her in the Mackintosh chair, while they continue deep in conversation. She is holding a glass of cordial, which she drains and places on the desk as Mr Sebastian leaves the room for a few moments.

I place my own drained glass on my coffee table, conscious of the parallel.

When he returns he is carrying several bolts of silken fabric, different pastel colours, a few vivid ones, all expertly chosen to match his client's complexion. She fingers each one reverently, deep in thought. Then she points to one of palest mauve, which she evidently finds soft and attractive.

Mr Sebastian rolls the other bolts up and places them in the corner of the room, ready to be taken back down to the shop.

Then he takes a pair of scissors and cuts a swatch of the fabric his client has selected. He strokes the square against her cheek, and then holds it against her lips. She sits very still, letting him play with her in this way.

Eventually he leans to kiss his client, with unhurried grace, through the chiffon fabric. Her face turns upwards like a flower, expectant, hungry for more as his lips travel down the silk to explore her pale neck.

I am shocked. Maybe this is no client, but a lover, or fiancé, even, picking out her trousseau, enjoying a stolen afternoon with the one she loves. I fight the stab of jealousy this brings as she shrugs off her jacket and begins to unbutton her blouse.

Surely she is just a client, I reason to myself, or I would have seen her before, being intimate with him? But this must be a special client, one he has known for many years, one he has had a relationship with. She has the look of one who wishes to rekindle something they have shared before.

I watch as she teases Mr Sebastian. She takes an age to unhook each button on her blouse, watching his expression with a look of defiance that barely masks her hunger for him. Something tells me they have indeed done this before; I wonder if she then betrayed her need for him too easily, and this time she wants to keep the upper hand. Well, that's what we voyeurs do; embroider the scenarios we are lucky enough to stumble upon.

She slowly shrugs out of her blouse. Her bra cups small round breasts. Even from here I can see the fabric is fine lace, the very best designer lingerie, in a pale conch colour, ruched to flattering effect. No doubt she knew he would appreciate such things, because his long fingers reach out to reverently brush the fabric moulding to the breast beneath.

After a short while, impatient for his touch on her

skin, she unhooks her bra, and lets it fall to one side. She arches her back to display those pale, perfect breasts, and her rosy nipples are firm with desire.

I kneel closer to my window, rapt with attention. I can feel my nipples swell in response to the way Mr Sebastian strokes her breasts, rolls her nipples between his fingers, bends to kiss and lick and nibble them.

His client remains perfectly still, but her lips part with pleasure and her delicate shoulders rise and fall in little sighs at Mr Sebastian's ministrations.

Again I get the sense they've played this game before.

Next Mr Sebastian kneels before the woman as she shrugs out of her knickers and trousers to display long legs, delicate blonde fuzz between them hiding her coral sex. A woman aware of her body, she is still wearing her high-heeled boots. She rests them in Mr Sebastian's lap, and scrapes the spiked heels gently along his inner thigh, against his groin, as he stoops to kiss her ankle, her knee, her thigh, her swelling cunt.

At this she throws her head back and moans, wrapping her legs around Mr Sebastian's torso, digging her heels into his back. He still wears his linen jacket, but he must feel the rake of those spikes and he seems to like it as he feasts between her legs.

I can almost feel the heat of his breath on my own sex, and I grow wet watching them. I let the silken folds of my kimono creep between my legs and I gently ease back and forth against its slippery silkiness, feeling nectar ooze from my sex as my own clit swells.

Mr Sebastian stands up, takes up the scissors once more, and cuts a few long strips of the delicate mauve silk.

She sits up straight and offers her wrists, neatly placed together, with charming eagerness. He takes them and he binds them expertly with a strip of silk. Then he ties her wrists loosely to a cross bar that hangs from the low ceiling. She writhes a little in protest but I can tell she loves it, the way he is testing her out, taking her to new places. After some discussion he gives her a silken blindfold.

Now that she is blinded, Mr Sebastian and I are both voyeurs to her naked body, the blush across her breasts, the quivering of her belly. She parts her lips, runs a tongue along them in nervous expectation, but she does not say anything. She is content to be admired, to feel his eyes upon her, to wait for whatever he is moved to accomplish with her.

I wonder if she can sense that more than one person is feasting on the sight of her. I want to kiss those vulnerable lips, twist those stiff nipples and lick her teasingly around her sex. I'm impatient to see what Mr Sebastian will choose to do.

He has more self-control than me. Slowly he wraps a swathe of silk around her breasts, and again he licks and nips at the flesh, the aching nipples, through the soft fabric.

I rub and stroke my own breasts, tweak my own nipples, through the fabric of my kimono, moaning with delight as the silk adds to the open abandonment of my skin and body to these caresses. I envy Mr Sebastian's client, feeling his lips and tongue and teeth as well as his fingertips. I want to bend and lick my own nipples, which I can just about do, but that would mean tearing my eyes away from the lovers across the little square.

And this I simply cannot bear to do, voyeur that I am.

Mr Sebastian takes another swatch of silk and binds it cunningly around the waist, thighs and hips of his captive, so that a length of soft fabric crosses her sex. It looks like a Japanese rite of bondage, designed to constrain gently yet give ultimate pleasure. Again he strokes her here, and kisses her there, and uses his fingers to gently torment her through the silk, so that she is at his tender mercy. He even strokes her clitoris with his index finger, and unexpectedly ploughs the silk inside of her while she spreads her knees wide and seems to beg for more.

I writhe gently in my longing, fingers finding my own sex, stroking through the kimono's silk.

Mr Sebastian abruptly stops what he is doing. The woman is panting, she seems to entreat him to continue, but he backs away, circling her, watching the quiver of her skin beneath the silk. Eventually he kneels before her and takes off her high-heeled boots, and wraps a separate strip of silk around each bare foot. Slowly he strokes and nibbles each toe, each ankle arch, while his client sways and moans softly, brought to the brink and left waiting for more.

I cannot see his face but I imagine his enjoyment, his sense of bringing his lover to the point of total abandonment by exquisite torture with his precious silk. The client bends her head to one side and seems to beg, in earnest supplication. The game must have proceeded to the next round. Mr Sebastian then undresses, leaving his clothes upon the leather chair beside his desk.

His body is lithe and well honed, dense with healthy muscle and bone and sinew. I can see even from here that his penis is fully erect. There is dark hair around his balls, across his chest and forearms that accentuates the smooth warm tones of his skin. I can see the muscles in his back and buttocks flex as he turns to stand above the woman, as he trains his cock against her lips. Gracious in his bounty at last.

She opens her mouth to eagerly embrace the swollen glans; the morsel she had obviously begged to receive is now delivered gently, tantalisingly. She is powerless against the rhythm and thrust he chooses, and he seems to choose exceedingly well. She licks his shaft and balls and lets her lips slide down, all the way down, with absolute abandon. I crane to get a better view, and my tongue travels across my lips when I wonder how that must feel, how Mr Sebastian's cock must taste. I long to accept the full weight of it in my mouth.

I moan with frustration.

Then Mr Sebastian pulls away and takes yet another strip of the exquisite silk, draping it around his genitals. He spits on his fingers and then dampens the diaphanous material so it clings to his contours. He returns to his client so that she can give fellatio through the silken fabric, which she proceeds to do in earnest.

I moisten and then bruise my lips upon the sleeve of my kimono, taste the flesh of the inside of my wrist through the slick silk, in an attempt to feel something of what she must feel, what he must feel.

It feels good. It heightens every sense of touch, addictive and languorous as opium, until I feel hot with desire yet tranquil with sensuous pleasure at the same time – an exquisite knife-edge of longing and procrastination.

Eventually Mr Sebastian pulls away from his lover's lips, and I wonder if he has come. But he has evidently bypassed the point of orgasm and, with some tantric stamina, still holds himself erect, his balls tight, poised to ejaculate.

He unfolds the silk, to reveal his arched, glistening erection, and he pulls his lover up so that she can turn around. Then she bends over, still tethered, as Mr Sebastian strokes her buttocks before he takes her from behind, through the soft film of silk, now wet with her juices, that still shrouds her sex.

She is crying out with the ecstasy, and that he has to hold her hips steady against the sudden onslaught of orgasm as he fucks gently, expertly, for maximum effect.

I plough my fingers through the damp silk of my kimono into my sweet swollen cunt and massage my clit, sliding the silk against me and inside me until I am in a frenzy, until finally I allow myself to cry out with sweet orgasmic release as the couple in the office opposite fuck themselves into coming.

After our mutual climax I watch, slowly stroking myself to cessation, as Mr Sebastian unbinds his client, and they both dress.

Then she becomes quite businesslike. She confirms her order for the silk, takes out her pocket book from her purse and writes him a cheque. I wonder if it includes hidden extras for services rendered. He watches her, detached and considerate, although I detect a trace of amusement on his face.

Moments later she is at the shop door, shaking hands and bidding polite farewell to Mr Sebastian. They both look well groomed and calm, as though nothing untoward has taken place. Then she hails a cab and is gone.

I wonder how many private appointments of this sort go on behind the lowered blinds and the locked door of Mr Sebastian's office. Quite a few, judging from the activity I have seen. But why did he conduct this particular 'interview' without lowering the blinds, so I could see everything clearly, when he was usually so discreet?

Before he goes inside the shop, Mr Sebastian looks up at my window once more and this time smiles directly at me. Even if he cannot see me now, because I lurk in the shade, he is confident that I am still there, watching him.

I have to reach the conclusion he has conducted this particular session of business with me in mind.

A few days later I am walking past the shop when Mr Sebastian suddenly emerges, shaking hands with a well-dressed American woman who saunters towards Oxford Street as though eager to indulge in more shopping. I falter, swerve to avoid them and the ankle strap of my left sandal gives way.

I curse softly and hover unsteadily on one high-heeled sandal while I examine the broken strap. I take both sandals off, decide it would be best to walk the final stretch home barefoot rather than try to rig a repair, when someone brushes my elbow.

'May I help you?' Mr Sebastian asks in a slow sonorous voice.

I feel a jolt of pleasure, and also a frission of fear. This man may be mad, bad and dangerous to know, as well as an incredible and sensuous lover. I must be cautious.

'It's nothing. My sandal strap is broken.'

'It's not good to walk the city pavements barefoot. Let me help you.'

'Please don't trouble yourself. I only live across the way,' I mumble, feeling a strange guilt as I look at his well-manicured hands, which I have seen do such outrageous and seductive things.

'I know. You have been my neighbour for a while now, yes? I am glad of the opportunity to finally make your proper acquaintance.' My nervous smile falters as his grows. He knows, he must know, how I have watched him. I feel that he can tell what I am thinking, how my body is feeling, tense and expect-ant with longing at his closeness.

'Please come into the shop, and I'll see if I can make a temporary repair to your sandal. If you like, I can show you around a little. You seem like the kind of woman who may appreciate fine silks.'

I blush and nod. I have no strength to resist such a gentle, teasing invitation. From the way I smile, that must be obvious.

'Very well. Thank you,' I manage to say at last.

Inside, the shop is simple and elegant, with comfortable leather chairs, a heavy coffee table of dark wood and brass. There are a few samples of coloured silks on a low counter, thick books of sam-ple swatches, and a vast tree of silk scarves tied to a central pole which glistens and dances in the sunlight.

There is also a reception desk in one corner where a pretty young brunette sits leafing through a catalogue. She glances up, smiles.

'It is all right, Jasmine, I shall attend to this customer. You may wish to take your coffee break now.'

Jasmine nods her thanks, collects her handbag and leaves to have her break in the nearby café with a friend. I know this, for I have seen her there on many occasions. The shop bell tinkles as she closes the door. Mr Sebastian and I are alone.

He selects one of the scarves from the pole, one made of smooth saffron silk.

'Sit down,' he says, and I obey. He kneels easily before me, graceful for such a tall man. He cradles my foot on his lap as he takes the broken sandal from me, slips it back on to my bare foot, and deftly wraps the scarf around my ankle, weaving it around the leather straps of the sandal, binding it to my foot.

His touch is gentle and makes me tingle. The silk is soft and warm against my bare skin. I find myself holding my breath as the silk merchant cradles my foot against his warm leg in those linen trousers. His long fingers wrap around my ankle bone to check the binding is secure, but not too tight, before he ties a neat bow in the silk scarf.

This triggers memories of my voyeuristic enjoyment, and I try not think about them, or the sheer sensual pleasure this arouses. I want to stroke his thighs with the heel of my sandals, tease his balls through the linen of his trousers ... my leg is trembling with the urge to do it, and with my determination to resist.

'Thank you,' I say throatily. 'I'll return the scarf tomorrow.'

I am stunned as his palm gently follows the arch of my foot, brushes admiringly against my bare toes, the nails which are painted silver-pink. He is slow to surrender his gentle grip on my ankle.

'There is really no need,' he reassures me pleasantly, 'Consider it a neighbourly gift.'

I could swear that he gently guides the spiky heel of my sandal across his crotch as he surrenders my left foot.

Before I have a chance to object he takes my other foot, replaces the right sandal, carefully buckles the leather strap, and again softly caresses the bare toes, the high arch of my foot, with reverential fingertips.

This time I surrender to the urge and let my heel dig a little into his thigh, scraping against the slight bulge in his crotch, and I see the flicker of appreciation in his eyes.

'Would you like to see the silks?' he asks softly, acknowledging my signal.

'Yes, please,' I whisper, before I have a chance to think. After all, I am in Aladdin's cave at last and I want to see just how far he is willing to go, and just how far I am willing to let him. This is, I suppose, the final temptation of all voyeurs.

I wonder how long Jasmine will spend on her tea break, and whether she will surprise us doing ... what?

'Come through to the next room,' he says, clearing his throat, betraying a hint of command. As I walk across the wooden floor, hips swinging to keep my balance in case the scarf suddenly gives way, I am conscious of Mr Sebastian watching my figure. And I glow with a reciprocal desire. It feels good to be the one being watched for a change. Maybe Mr Sebastian is tired of letting me play the voyeur, and maybe I am too.

The silk scarf feels smooth as moonstone, warm as his skin, against my ankle bone, and I already feel hot and eager for more.

The next room contains shelves with bolts of luminous silks stacked high to the ceiling. In the centre of the room is a broad, wide table for laying out the material and cutting lengths to be made up into kimonos, dresses, whatever the client desires. There are stacks of pattern books in the corner, an array of scissors and measuring rules ... and a full-length mirror, where clients hold the silks against their body, their hair, and check that the colour suits them.

I glance at myself. My legs are long, somehow glossier, with the addition of the saffron silk around my left ankle bone. My summer blouse, my linen skirt, look suddenly superfluous. All I want to wear are my sandals, and some silk. My shining eyes, my moist parted lips, betray this thought to me. I look like one of Vermeer's women, watched and waiting, hoping the worst may happen.

I glance back to the silks, guilty fantasies racing through my head, while Mr Sebastian watches me with a half-smile on his lips.

'Which silk do you like?' he asks me as I travel the shelves stroking the bolts of colour that take my eye.

I pause at a warm ginger-saffron, which almost matches the scarf he has wrapped around my ankle. Somehow it glows against my pale skin, giving it lustre, and I sense that it matches the highlights in my chestnut hair. It also feels warm, inviting, like softest eiderdown against my fingertips.

'Good choice,' he compliments me, and takes this bolt of silk down to lay on the counter, unfolding an ample length.

I smooth it with my palms and the backs of my wrists. It is so soft, so smooth, so yielding and sensual. I want to be wrapped in the gossamer lightness of its erotic cocoon.

'It is very lovely,' I whisper conspiratorially.

'It is one of our most expensive silks, handwoven in China, hand-dyed in Tibet. Here, hold it against you.'

I stand in front of the mirror while he wraps a sinuous fold of fabric around my bare shoulders.

I look like a different woman. I look like the type of woman he would desire, who would do unspeakable things in the back of a silk shop on a summer's afternoon.

I clear my throat, suddenly nervous. I do not know what to do while he looks at me with his large brown eyes, appraising me, my curves of breast and hip, made so obvious beneath the saffron fabric.

'Wait there,' he orders, and returns with a large pair of silver scissors.

With one swift, shearing motion he cuts free the fabric entwining me, and I know that he has decided, and I am glad.

I gather the silk more closely to me now.

'It feels good, doesn't it?' Mr Sebastian says. 'It feels even better against totally naked skin.'

There is a challenge in his voice, in the amber glint of his dark eyes.

I continue to look at him as I slowly undo my skirt, letting it fall. I shrug out of my blouse, and let that fall too.

Mr Sebastian clears his throat and continues watching me.

I undo my bra, and struggle out of my panties. Now I am naked except for my high-heeled sandals and his saffron silk.

'You're right,' I say briefly. 'It feels heavenly.'

There is a pause, and I wonder if I have been too forward, betrayed my need for him too easily, like I imagined the willowy blonde once did. But from the way his eyes feast on me I know he is enjoying my nakedness beneath the exclusive silk.

'I am so glad you decided to come in,' he whispers at last. 'I have often watched you going to and from your work, stopping to look in the window, and I thought you would look so beautiful, wrapped just so in saffron silk. May I touch you?'

'Yes,' I whisper.

I feel as though I am a statue, worshipped by his fingers that stroke and follow every curve of my body through the material. I am afraid to move and spoil the moment. I revel in the way his long fingers toy with my nipples, and stroke between my legs, and test the mettle of my inner thighs and my calves, and softly stroke the nape of my neck, until I am resonating to his touch like a fine-bred filly.

I gasp with surprise when finally he kneels and licks at my mound, nibbling my clitoris through the warm saffron. His tongue is gentle and precise, teasing me to full arousal, unhurried and generous in its voyage of discovery through my inner folds. My breath shortens; I take little gasps, tug at his dark hair as he begins to gently probe inside me, holding me steady with a firm grasp on my buttocks. His palms brand me through the soft delicate stuff that encases my limbs.

It seems the most natural thing in the world to let him pick me up, lay me on the counter, explore me like I was a banner of his most precious fabric. When he unzips his fly, releases his erect penis, I finger it gratefully, and its silken ridges are warm and solid. My cunt is wet for him as he slides gently in, balancing my buttocks on the edge of the counter while he stands between my spread-eagled legs.

We are by this stage both trembling, clinging to each other with strange vertigo and sensuous need, hurrying to climax before we are disturbed. My sex spasms and its innermost spot quivers to welcome him further into me. He fits so perfectly. We rock and wave against each other like silken flags in a warm breeze until the orgasm, soft and satiating as cinnamon sugar, runs its course.

We hear the shop doorbell tinkle. Jasmine has returned from her tea break.

Mr Sebastian smiles, puts a finger to his lips and reluctantly withdraws.

I dress with haste, while he tidies away the bolts. The length he cut, which we have used in our love-making, is still pooled on the table, and I wonder what he will do with it. Keep it as a souvenir?

When I am ready, Mr Sebastian escorts me back through the shop, nodding to Jasmine, and opens the door onto the sunny street, treating me with the same respect I have seen him show to his other clients. I am grateful that he keeps it all so calm and natural. He seems in no hurry to dismiss me. He shakes my hand politely, holds onto it a few moments longer than necessary, making me tingle.

'Well, thank you. For everything,' I say uncertainly.

'You are most welcome. So, when can you drop by my office for an appointment? Would Thursday at five p.m. suit you?'

'An appointment? In your office?' I ask, feeling a little dizzy at this sudden invitation.

'I think that the saffron would look most becoming on you as a simple dress for the summer, but I'll need you to try it on in case I have not remembered your measurements exactly. And of course we'll need to discuss the appropriate payment.'

I stare at him a moment and he raises on eyebrow slightly, a ghost of a smile on his lips. Again there is a glint of challenge in his dark eyes.

I smile in return. After all, I have always wanted to purchase a bespoke silk dress, ever since I first paused in front of his shop window. And I have always wanted to be invited into his office, ever since I saw him there with that willowy blonde.

How easily he has read my mind.

'Thursday at five would be perfect. I look forward to it,' I reply.

'And I will enjoy seeing to your needs, as my new favourite client.'

I'll let you know how the dress turns out. I am sure it will be very beautiful and fit me perfectly.

As does Mr Sebastian, purveyor of silks.

Seams and Ladders
Fiona Locke

When he doesn't get off at Tottenham Court Road I know he is following me. And when he meets my eyes with that unnerving frankness, I realise he wants me to know.

Several seats become available as the train disgorges its passengers, but he remains standing. Right in front of me. He's tall, with silver-flecked hair and dark compelling eyes. Elegantly dressed in a sombre, old-fashioned suit. And about twice my age. Against my will my eyes flick upwards and I avert them quickly when I see he's still looking at me.

He had been there on the platform almost every day, watching me. Not ogling. No, his scrutiny was more like a military inspection than a prurient leer. I had the sense that I was on parade and I felt myself standing just a little straighter, a little taller.

He always got off with me a few stops later, at Tottenham Court Road. Then we would go our separate ways once we were above ground. And while his brooding gaze excited me, it was always a relief to escape its intensity.

But today I remained in my seat as we reached our station. And he didn't get off either.

The train rockets through the subterranean labyrinth, carrying me away from the bookshop where I work. My boss will not be pleased.

Its brakes shrieking, the train shudders to a halt at Oxford Circus and this time he does make a move. But it's only to sit down – directly opposite me. The carriage is nearly empty. I glance at the doors and debate whether I should get off and double back. I wonder if my companion will do the same. But something makes me stay.

The doors close like a promise withdrawn and I feel exposed by his bold stare. My decision to stay suddenly seems reckless – an offer I'm not sure I'm prepared to make. I shift in my seat, fidgeting. My nylons whisper nervously as I cross my legs and I see him smile to himself, as though they've imparted a secret to him.

I tug feebly at the hem of my too-short skirt, flushed with warmth at the sense of exposure. He makes no secret of staring at my legs. Normally I welcome the attention. Even at work. *Especially* at work. After all, it's the reason I dress the way I do: a cross between air hostess and librarian. I wear my long blonde hair pulled back, a few wisps framing my face appealingly. Just a whiff of suppressed sexuality.

I've always been an incorrigible flirt and I know how to display myself to be admired. This man is no different from any other I taunt and tease. I could see he liked my legs, so my hemlines got higher. So did my heels.

But that was when *I* was in control. Now he's raised the stakes. Now *he* is the hunter.

Bond Street. When I see he still has no intention of getting up I make as if to rise myself. He tilts his head with an expression of amused curiosity, his sensual mouth curling in a knowing smile. I feel toyed with. I don't like having the tables turned. It's like forgetting all the steps to a dance I choreographed myself.

I stand up hurriedly, stumbling in my heels, and reach the doors a second too late. They hiss shut in front of me, trapping me. Chagrined, I turn my back on him. Unease coils around me as I sense his eyes, exploring me like a stranger's hand. I pretend to rummage in my bag for something, a pathetically transparent ruse.

'You've got a ladder in your stocking.'

His presumption shocks me and I stand immobile, not knowing how to respond.

'How very careless,' he tuts.

I round on him. 'It's your fault. If you hadn't . . .'

Hadn't what? Looked at what I was flaunting? I turn away again in a huff.

The plastic seat creaks as he stands up. I've provoked him. The hairs on the back of my neck rise, tingling. His trousers brush my calf and I stand like a statue, my stillness inviting more. I can hardly breathe. When I feel his hand in the small of my back I gasp, but don't move.

'You should be more careful,' he continues, his posh accent low and silky in my ear. I close my eyes, shivering at the feel of his warm breath on my neck. The hand slides lower, until it rests on my bottom. My cheeks clench involuntarily and the hand creeps another inch lower.

I grip the hanging strap above me tightly to steady myself against the rocking motion of the train as the hand slides down the back of my left thigh.

'It's just here,' he says, pressing his finger gently against the little hollow behind my knee. 'I expect you snagged it getting up in such a rush.'

The reproachful tone weakens me. I don't really care about the stockings. They're only an inexpensive Lycra blend, after all – some cheap multipack buy. I have others. But the rebuke insists I acknowledge the damage. Shifting my weight to my right leg, I turn the left one in, twisting it to look down at the desecrated black material. Anticipating a huge tear, I'm surprised when I see it's only a tiny run.

'Is that all?' I laugh. 'It's nothing hairspray or nail varnish can't patch.'

His face looks like a priest's in response to blasphemy. A perfectionist, then. A connoisseur who knows exactly what he likes and expects it to be immaculately presented. My stomach flutters.

I don't even notice when the train stops again. The doors whoosh open and a few people push past us into the carriage. I look at the platform, debating. Neither of us moves. The doors close on Marble Arch and the train lurches into motion again, heading steadily westwards.

'I'll send you a new pair,' he says coolly. 'If you'll wear them to dinner with me.'

He speaks with the effortless confidence of one accustomed to getting what he wants. Determined not to feel humbled, I search my mind for some cheeky rejoinder. Nothing comes. My hesitation only secures his advantage.

He leans in to whisper, 'And when I say wear them, I mean wear them *properly*.'

He says it with a gravity that implies more than just keeping the seams straight, but I don't have the breath to question it. I press my legs together at the tacit threat. The thought of being subjected to his exacting scrutiny fills me with both dread and desire.

'OK,' I say at last, my voice a meek little squeak.

I'm expecting something black, but he surprises me. The stockings are flesh-toned, a colour I've never owned. What's the point of leg-coloured stockings when you can just go bare?

The stockings shimmer as I shake them out of the packaging and admire them. I have never seen anything so sheer in my life. They're pure nylon and utterly weightless – like cobweb. I finger the material with fascination, drawing it across the back of my arm.

A seam runs down the back of each stocking to meet the pointed tip of the French heel. The maker's lavish white signature decorates the top welt, which is doubled over and sewn in the back with a small finishing hole – something I've only ever seen in old pictures.

At first I'm certain that the stockings are too big. However, when I hook my thumbs into the welt and begin gathering the material into a roll I realise that they don't stretch at all; they're exactly the length of my legs. He has a sharp eye.

I point my right foot and slide it into the stocking, gently unrolling it and drawing it up my leg. The silky sensation is an unexpected delight. So these are 'proper' nylons. I suddenly understand what all the fuss is about.

I clip the garters into place, twisting round in the mirror to straighten the seam. A perfect fit. My leg is encased in glass. It shines and gleams in the light. The reinforced heel and toe resemble a ballet slipper and I point my toes, showing off my high-arched insteps in the mirror.

Eager to see the whole effect, I gather up the other stocking and dip my toes into it. But as I tug the nylon up and over my knee it catches on a ragged fingernail. I gasp in dismay and disentangle the filaments that have pulled loose.

I don't want to look, but I have to. And sure enough, where the nylon has snagged is a puckered little line like a cat scratch. Right across the top of the thigh. I smooth the threads down, but the imperfection stands out like a spill of ink on a wedding dress.

Bugger.

I close my eyes in a moment of childish desperation, praying that when I open them the line will be gone. It doesn't work.

Maybe it's not as bad as I fear. I look up at my reflection, pulling the stocking tight and examining it. No, it's every bit as bad as I fear. And while such a rip wouldn't bother *me*, there is no way it will pass muster with *him*.

Dejectedly I look at the clock. I still have an hour. There might be time to sort it out.

I peel myself out of the stockings and dress for dinner. A short slinky little black velvet number with a pearl choker. Black strappy Roman sandals with stiletto heels. A bit goth, a bit glam. But it showcases my legs, which is what he wants to see. In proper nylons.

Ruined proper nylons in hand, I deliver myself

into the mercy of the nearest upmarket lingerie shop. I feel like a desperate parent furtively trying to replace a child's dead pet, but it has to be done.

With a sympathetic wince, the matronly woman behind the counter tells me sadly that they don't stock vintage nylons.

'Vintage?' I repeat, feeling ill.

'Oh yes, these are the real thing,' she says, holding them admiringly in her manicured hands. 'Authentic. Nineteen-forties. Marlene Dietrich might have worn these. They're lovely, aren't they?'

I feel as though I've eaten a raw egg. I put my head down on the counter.

'We do have reproductions,' she assures me. 'I'm not sure we can find you an exact match, but we might have something that looks close enough.'

I raise my head, my eyes wide with hope.

She takes my hand in both of hers and pats it as though consoling a grieving friend. 'Come on, love, let's have a look.'

It's nearly an hour later that I leave the shop wearing the nearest thing she could find. I wouldn't know the difference. I can only hope he won't either.

His approving smile as I walk towards the table calms my jangling nerves.

'You look lovely,' he says.

I release the breath I've been holding and sink into the chair. 'Thank you.'

He offers me a glass of wine and looks down at my lap. I cross my legs obligingly and the nylon gives a soft rustle. I sit with my legs out to the side to give him a better view.

'How do they feel?' he asks.

'Silky,' I say at once, remembering the first pair. These ones aren't nearly as fine. 'They're barely there.'

He smiles.

Encouraged, I cross them again to tease him, pointing my toe and raising my leg, showing off like a sex kitten. He edges his chair closer to me and I place one foot on his knee. His hand slides over my instep and up the length of my sleek glossy leg. The transparent barrier enhances the caress and my sex grows warmer in response. His eyes darken as he traces a finger along my calf and I wonder nervously if the seams are straight. Blushing, I withdraw my leg.

'They're very nice,' he says at last.

Relieved, I take a sip of wine.

'But how did the ones *I* sent you feel?'

The wine becomes a solid lump and I force it down with a loud swallow. My cheeks burn as I drag my gaze back up to meet his. What can I possibly say?

Slowly he rises from the table, just as the waitress arrives to take our order. He takes my hand and addresses the surprised girl. 'I'm terribly sorry, but I'm afraid it's just the wine. Something's come up and we'll have to leave.'

I'm speechless as she takes his money and abandons us. Finally I find my voice. 'You're not serious!'

But the cool gleam in his eyes assures me that he is. 'I did say you were to wear them properly,' he reminds me. 'And you're not wearing them at all.'

His frown makes me tremble with more than fear. I know there will be a reckoning before the night is over.

'Look, I . . .' My feeble protest peters out under his

piercing stare. I bite my lip, blushing. He can see exactly what his censorious tone is doing to me.

'Juliet.'

I squirm at the way he makes my name sound like a reprimand.

'What?'

'Tell me why you aren't wearing what I sent you.'

I blush. 'I snagged them.'

He gathers my hands and looks pointedly at my chewed fingernails. 'I'm not surprised.'

Abashed, I pull them away, shoving them out of sight behind my back.

'Where *are* the ones I sent you?'

'In my bag.' I hadn't dared to throw them away, even though they were ruined.

At his expectant look I fumble the clasp open and hand over the wispy nylon, cringing as though relinquishing contraband to a customs officer.

He shakes his head over them before tucking them into his pocket. 'Right. You have a choice. You can come with me and rectify the situation. Or you can go home.'

He makes me feel like a naughty child. I can be sent to bed without supper or I can stay up and play grown-up games. My knees are weak.

As my stomach gives a plaintive grumble I whisper, 'OK. I'll go with you.'

The shop is a shrine to vintage glamour. Mannequins with hourglass figures model the fashions of bygone eras while a warbling voice sings an old wartime tune on a scratchy turntable. Pictures of screen goddesses adorn the walls: Rita Hayworth, Louise Brooks, Audrey Hepburn.

'Sorry, we're just closing!' comes a perky American voice from the back of the shop.

A door opens and a young Bettie Page lookalike scampers out, high heels clicking on the floor. A leopard-print party frock flares out below her knees and her heels are so high I marvel that she can walk at all. She stops short, grinning flirtatiously at my companion. 'Mr Allardyce!' she exclaims. 'Such a pleasure to see you again so soon!'

I realise that I have never even asked his name, though I'd given him mine, along with my address. He's made me reckless.

'Elaine,' he says, smiling. 'Look what I've brought you to play with.'

As I blink in confusion, he gestures ostentatiously, presenting me like an offering.

Elaine looks me up and down. 'Oh yes,' she says, nodding her head with the enthusiasm of an artist asked to perform. 'This the one you bought the stockings for?'

I chew my lip.

'Yes,' he says heavily. 'Only I think I'd like to see the full effect.'

'Always my pleasure, Mr Allardyce.' She gives me a last appraising look while I try to puzzle out the 'always'. 'What a delightful surprise.'

I'm just a piece in a museum collection. A piece in need of restoration. Nervously I turn to him, a worried question in my eyes.

'Don't worry,' he says in a voice that does nothing to reassure me. 'When Elaine is finished with you you'll hardly recognise yourself.'

She grins and releases my hair from its clasp. 'The gentleman knows what he likes,' she says, addressing the comment to him in a tone that tells me it's an inside joke. She hasn't spoken to me once.

My eyes widen. I came here thinking this was about replacing a pair of stockings. But he has far more in mind. At the same time the fear of the unknown is exhilarating. And the way they're discussing me ... It objectifies me. It pushes the same buttons as being stalked on the Underground. I can feel my knickers growing damp as I surrender. My silence is consent.

Elaine takes my hand and leads me towards the back of the shop. I cast a glance over my shoulder in time to see Mr Allardyce lock the door and turn the CLOSED sign around.

He's right. Two hours later I hardly recognise myself. My hair cascades over my shoulders in glorious 1940s waves. Deep-red lips and smouldering bedroom eyes transform my face into a vision from the silver screen. The impeccable cut of the charcoal-grey suit gives me an enviable wasp waist. And the tight pencil skirt makes my long legs seem even longer.

'Perfection,' he declares, admiring Elaine's handiwork. 'Absolute perfection.'

She beams proudly. 'Thank you, Mr Allardyce.'

He turns to me at last. 'Now we can go to dinner.'

Captivated by the glamorous stranger in the mirror, I can't resist pulling 'come hither' faces while he and Elaine agree on a price behind me. The figure makes me gulp, but I don't let it show. The gentleman knows what he likes.

'Oh, I almost forgot,' he says. 'She'll need a new pair of stockings too.'

I feel like Eliza Doolittle at the embassy ball. Will my accent be his next project?

I draw stares back at the restaurant, but I enjoy the attention. I'm also grateful he's finally decided to let me eat. I'm starving.

He has me sit with my legs on display. Sheathed in vintage nylons. Seams straight. No ladders.

Afterwards the black cab takes us to a cobbled mews near the V&A. As he leads me into his immaculate terraced house it suddenly occurs to me to wonder what he's doing on the westbound Central line every morning.

He offers me wine and directs me to an elaborately carved Victorian sofa in front of the fireplace. My eyes scan the room, taking in its elegant but tasteful furnishings. He sits to my left, positioning me to afford himself the best leg show, indulging his predilection as well as my vanity. His eyes roam from my toes to my hair, drinking in every detail.

'You're the quintessential vamp,' he says. 'You were born in the wrong decade.'

It's a peculiar compliment, but undeniably true. I stretch my legs out across his lap and he strokes them. He pinches the nylon between his thumb and forefinger, pulling it out away from my skin and letting it fall back. I'm surprised at the way the stockings crease at my knees and ankles, where the nylon isn't taut.

Lifting my right ankle, he unlaces the shoe and slips it off, cradling my warm satiny foot in his hands before releasing it.

'You do have lovely feet.'

No one's ever told me that before. I'm flattered. And now I want to play.

Intent on gaining the upper hand, I press the ball of my foot into his crotch. He begins to stiffen immediately. I had hoped to outmanoeuvre him by making the first move, but he isn't taken aback by my forwardness. Redoubling my efforts, I grind my foot against him, caressing him through his trousers.

When I offer him the other foot he strips it of its shoe as well. The sandal falls to the floor with a soft thud. I place both feet on the growing bulge in his trousers and he sighs contentedly as I curl my toes against his hardness. I tease him, rubbing my legs against one another and enjoying the sibilant hiss of nylon. My sex responds to his arousal as well, moistening in anticipation.

But the stimulation doesn't ruffle his composure. With impossible nonchalance he says, 'I've been watching you, you know.'

Something in his smile belies the innocence of the comment. My legs cease their manipulations as the penny drops. He isn't referring to the Tube journeys; he's been to the bookshop where I work. He's seen the smut I sell, flashing the customers a coy grin and a glimpse of cleavage. He knows what a prickteaser I am. He's probably even followed me home, tracing my commute back from the shop. It would be creepy if it wasn't so erotic.

'Now then,' he says, interrupting my epiphany. 'We have some unfinished business to take care of.'

'We have?'

'Your carelessness.'

Oh. That.

He raises my legs like a gate and gets to his feet. I

can't guess what he has in mind as he retrieves one of my shoes and slips the leather lacing free of the grommets.

I giggle nervously. 'Is that so I can't run away?'

Ignoring my question, he runs his hands up the fronts of my shiny thighs and I moan softly at his touch. The tailored skirt clings to my legs and he snakes his fingers under the hem. When he reaches the garter clips he flicks them open with surprising skill, releasing the stockings. He's done this before. Many times.

'Lift up.'

I obey and his fingers slide underneath my legs to release the clips at the back. The nylon goes slack and he peels the stockings down one by one. My legs and feet tingle at their exposure to the air, sensitised from their silky bondage.

'On your back,' he says. 'Legs up.'

I'm embarrassed for him to see my feet so close up out of the stockings. I haven't had a pedicure in weeks and he doesn't hide his disapproval. I knew he was a perfectionist – how could I have let that slide? I should have painted my toenails at the very least.

Flustered, I lean back, raising my legs. I'm mesmerised by his control, the effortless way he has of putting me completely under a spell.

I look away as he draws the ruined stockings from his pocket. Without a word he takes my hands and crosses my wrists. Then he winds the stocking around them.

Blood pounds in my head. The position draws my knickers tight against my pulsing sex and I squeeze my legs together. I flush deeply as he pulls my arms over my head and secures them to the scrolled arm of the sofa. The position humbles me intensely and my legs begin to tremble with the effort of holding them up.

'Bend your knees.'

I do as he says and he strokes his thumbs over the balls of my feet, making me shiver. He wraps the other stocking around my knees, tying it securely.

'There are ways to punish naughty little feet,' he says, measuring his words. 'Feet that don't present themselves properly when instructed.'

Though his voice is low and seductive, there is something military about him, a natural authority that reduces me to quivering compliance. His demeanour promises punishment for every misstep. With slow deliberation he doubles the lacing from my sandal, then doubles it again, making a small whip of four looped lashes. He snaps it against his palm and I jump, imagining its bite against my vulnerable feet.

Pushing my bound knees against my chest, he holds my ankles in position as he raises the leather. He brings it down smartly across both feet and I gasp at the sharp sting. I strain against the stocking that binds my wrists, but the nylon is surprisingly strong. I'm not going anywhere.

He flicks the lacing across my tender soles again and I yelp and writhe. The helplessness is intoxicating and I abandon myself to the pain as another stroke falls. Then another. My feet are hypersensitive and the delicate skin tingles unbearably. But the feeling is exquisite. The tingling spreads up along my legs, awakening sensations I didn't know were possible. My body is alive with the delirious fusion of agony and bliss.

When at last the whipping stops I plead for more with my body, flexing my feet, presenting them. But he cups them in his hands and presses his lips against the burning, throbbing arches, stimulating me beyond endurance. I shudder as he drags his tongue along each sole, dipping it between my toes.

Panting, desperate, I throw my head back as his skilful tongue explores every inch of my punished feet. I barely even notice the hand untying the stocking at my knees. My legs fall open and he trails his fingers over my inner thighs, spreading me open even further. My gyrations cause my skirt to ruck up underneath me, revealing my soaked knickers. The throbbing, insistent urge between my legs is so intense it makes me light-headed.

With his tongue, he traces a path from my right thigh to my swollen sex. When I feel his hot breath against me I arch back, thrusting myself forwards in a wanton display. I feel like a wartime whore entertaining the troops, demanding satisfaction of my own. He pulls back to unzip himself and I gaze hungrily at his cock as he stands over me. I want him to take me. I want it rough, cruel, nasty.

But his game isn't over yet. Taking hold of my feet, he positions them on either side of his cock. Eager to please, I squeeze his length between my high arches, rolling and kneading the hard shaft. My soles feel every throb and twitch of his desire.

His breathing quickens and his eyes drift closed for a moment. But he opens them again immediately, returning his gaze to the naughty feet servicing him. I'm amazed he can stand. Balancing his cock on the instep of my left foot, I tease him with the toes of my right, a burlesque trick that comes naturally to me in my new incarnation.

I watch his face intently and see that he won't last long. I press my feet against him, hard, sliding them up and down the length, revelling in my brazen performance. The climax overtakes him and I position my feet to catch every hot jet of sperm as it dribbles across my insteps and between my toes.

My tormentor is pleased. A contented smile spreads across his face, crinkling the corners of his eyes. He parts my knees again and I close my eyes as he peels away my sodden knickers. He leaves them at half mast and I squirm, giving a little whimper. I can't wrap my legs around him; I have to hold them up. I can just imagine the picture I present – dolled up like a vintage screen siren and dishevelled from my lurid exhibition. My hands tied, my hair mussed and my knickers round my knees. Everything on display. Shameless.

I bite my lip when his fingers begin to stroke me, teasing the damp folds and deliberately avoiding the spot that will make me explode. I grind eagerly in response to his touch, begging for release. I'm unable to help myself with my hands restrained and he exploits my weakness fully. He teases me, dipping his fingers inside me and swirling them round. Finally, the torturous fingers converge on the hard little bud of my clit, brushing it lightly. The pleasure mounts astonishingly as he draws his fingers along the crease on either side, coaxing breathless cries from me until I'm ready to scream in frustration.

But then he stops. With a desperate moan I yank at my bonds, pleading with my eyes. His hands drift away from my sex and he slides my knickers to my ankles, taking his time, playing with me. At last he slips them off and I notice with surprise that his cock is already beginning to harden again. I marvel at his stamina, feeling even more defenceless and vulnerable.

When he moves to spread my legs I flex the muscles of my thighs, resisting. He exerts a little more force, prising my knees apart easily. I quiver as he kneels above me, his cock now fully erect. But I don't want to be passive. With a defiant smile I raise my right foot and plant it in the centre of his chest, pushing him back firmly.

But he is stronger than I am. He grasps both ankles deftly, wrenching my legs wide apart.

I gasp at the show of power and a wave of excitement flashes through me. The head of his cock demands entrance and I struggle as much as my position will allow, torturing myself by delaying it.

At last he drives himself inside, filling me up, pounding me with merciless force. I drown in my helplessness, crying out loudly with every hard thrust. It's too much for me. The deluge of sensations bursts throughout my body and I clamp my legs together around him, bucking and twisting as the spasms surge through me, assaulting me, overwhelming me, devastating me.

As I drift back down to earth, his features swim into focus. I manage a drunken lopsided smile, but speech is beyond me. He unties me and I wince at the pins and needles in my arms.

Before sending me home in a cab, he helps me tidy myself. He puts my new stockings in a carrier bag and inspects my fingers again, tutting at the jagged nails. 'You'll need a manicure, of course,' he tells me, arching an eyebrow warningly.

Of course.

I want to tell him I'm sorry I was a bad girl. Except that I'm not.

'Wear your new suit to work tomorrow,' he instructs, his eyes glittering. 'With proper nylons.'

Oh yes, the gentleman knows what he likes, all right.

But so do I.

I sit opposite him on the crowded train, dressed as ordered. I press my thighs together primly, enjoying the soft rustle that makes him smile. Slowly, I slide the hem of the skirt up over my knees, drawing it hissing over my thighs. As it creeps steadily towards the stocking tops I make sure he can see my fingers.

I watch him watching me, his eyes focused on the gleaming nylon. And slowly, deliberately, I place my hands on my knees. I curl my fingers like a hawk's talons, hooking my torn fingernails into the delicate material. His eyes widen slightly and I give him a sweet smile as I dig in and drag my nails up my thighs, tearing the stockings. Ruining them.

The expression on his face is well worth the price I'll pay for it tonight.

Fiona Locke's short stories have appeared in numerous Wicked Words collections. Her first novel, *Over the Knee*, is published by Nexus Enthusiast.

The All Night Tulsa Brown

Radio is a glamorous business – for about fifteen minutes. After that you realise it's low-paying, hierarchical and – in my small Midwestern city at least – sexist. The day shifts went to the men, the resonant bass-throated devils whose voices had been shaped by whiskey and cigarettes.

I got the city when it was asleep. I was Sherry Sharone, the velvet vixen on CHQT from midnight to six a.m, the shift we simply called the All Night. In some places that would have been fun; there's hot radio after the sun goes down. But my station was a paragon of easy listening, also known as Death by Syrup. If my audience wasn't already comatose, I was supposed to lull them into it.

'Glide, Sherry,' the programme director admonished me. 'You've got a good voice but you have to mellow your delivery. Pull up over them like a blanket, and quit being such a –'

'Live wire?' I said.

'Bitch.'

It was hard. I was frustrated. By two a.m. of my working night, my fantasies swung between riding a big cock against the wall of a thumping, throbbing dance club, and doing something unspeakable to every copy of 'My Heart Will Go On'.

The All Night didn't lend itself to a social life. What opportunities weren't squashed by my strange hours were ground under the station's 'rules of decorum'. At 27, I remembered my club days like a distant dream: a copper-coloured wash in my short, sandy hair and the twenty – or so – extra pounds swaying on my breasts and hips. On a dance floor I bounced, the distinctive female jiggle that swivelled men on their bar stools. I missed that, but even more I missed the thrill of a needy groan against my ear, desire on the verge of agony. 'Please, Sherry' always sent a stripe of lightning through my jeans.

My friends couldn't understand my current 'date difficulty'. 'Men phone you all the time. Well, at least on the request line.'

It made me sigh. There's a cardinal rule in radio: the listener is king – unless he wants to meet you. Then you have to assume he's a nut. It was a safety issue. We weren't allowed to respond to fan mail, and we had a video security system on the door. I even had a 'panic button' in the control booth, a silent alarm that would get the police over in two minutes, thirty-five seconds.

I appreciated that. Some of my fans were no-frills suitors whose calls never made it to air.

'Ah, c'mon, Sherry. I've got eight hard inches.'

'And it's attached to six feet of loser. Bad ratio, fella.' *Click.*

The 'Romeos' were even worse, perhaps because they were so devoted. Carl was indefatigable.

'I know how to treat a lady like you, Sherry.'

'I eat balls for breakfast, Carl.'

'I'm a great cook!'

Click.

In truth, I loved being on air. There's a heady

magic in getting paid to talk, like spinning straw into gold. To look out the big plate-glass window in the control booth at the twinkling city ignited something ravenous in me. I wanted to bewitch every listener, reel them in and hold them like stars in my hands.

And I discovered something: you can sail away on the stream of your own voice. It's like daydreaming while you drive. The words pour out in a smooth, effortless flow and your mind skips ahead, a flat stone over water. After eight months, my fantasies had pooled deep, fed by two springs, hunger and boredom.

But that wasn't like sex. One night in the middle of August the velvet vixen was feeling ragged, and getting punchy on the phone-line buttons.

'Hi, can I request a song?'

'No.'

'Hi, can I –'

'Nope.'

'Hey, could you play a song for me?'

I spun around in my chair. The man leaned in the doorway of the control booth, holding my garbage can and grinning. At the edge of my consciousness I registered his uniform: short-sleeved work shirt and canvas pants in denim blue. Cleaning company. I even remembered that I'd seen his wide back earlier, bent into the staff-room sink.

That hadn't prepared me for his front. He had a strong neck and square jaw, features that were more pronounced thanks to a marine-recruit haircut. This man looked *shorn*. He wasn't muscle bound, but broad shouldered and tight hipped, the devastating

V of a fine male body that spoke to my female parts in basic English, especially the part tucked high under my summer skirt.

His whole body tilted in a deferential way, like a ranch hand at the back door of the Big House, yet he gazed at me with bold familiarity. Had I met him somewhere? No, I wouldn't have forgotten this barroom buck.

My professional training had vanished. For long seconds I was speechless in the flush of heat and high-school goofiness. Damn, he was cute.

'No. No requests,' I blurted at last. In the corner of my eye, I noticed my digital countdown clock – this song was ending in eight seconds, and then I had concert tickets to give away. 'Get out.'

He lifted an eyebrow, and touched his forehead in a mock salute. 'Yes, *ma'am.*' He took my garbage can with him when he left.

Thank God I could have punched those buttons in my sleep and talked my way through an earthquake. The tickets went to caller number eight – other than that, I had only a vague idea what planet I was on.

Oh, that was classy, Sherry. A man walks through the door and you revert to monosyllables?

I felt the sting of a different regret, too. I'd been outright rude. Had I been doing the All Night so long I didn't know how to communicate with people, only talk *at* them? As soon as my next song set was in progress, I slipped out of the booth and went to find him.

He was vacuuming a hallway, intent on his work, strong shoulders and forearms swaying with easy grace as he manoeuvred the industrial-sized unit. Yet there was still something precise in his movements.

Military? I thought of the salute, sarcasm to be sure, yet so deft it made me think he'd practised.

I waved to get his attention. The vacuum's engine gargled to a stop.

'Look, I didn't mean to bark at you. It's just that we're in ratings right now. I have to stick to the Play List.'

'That's OK. I was just hoping for something with a *beat*.' He gave the hose a little back-and-forth shimmy, as if dancing with it. 'Besides, I've listened to your show a lot. I already knew you were –'

'A bitch?'

'Nobody's fool.' His smile was strangely shy, glimmering with a secret. 'Sherry Sharone *owns* the night.'

Bald flattery, and I didn't care. I tingled in the wash of the accolade.

'Well, drop by the booth when you have a minute. I'll see what I can do.'

Guests were absolutely forbidden in the control room. There was only one place he could stand upright and not be seen through the big window: the narrow space between two high bookshelves, directly across from the control board. His shoulders touched wood on either side and he had to flatten himself to the wall, a handsome, straight-armed toy soldier.

And soldier he was, part-time at least. Jeff was 24, a final-year engineering student who was a weekend reservist. That haircut was army, not marines. And he worked nights, too? It made me laugh and shake my head.

'Is there a single minute of your day that isn't planned out for you?' I asked.

'I like to push myself, see how much I can take.' That smile again, the private one.

I glanced at the clock. 'Well, push yourself to hold still for thirty seconds. I'm going to turn on the microphone and you can't breathe, blink or fart until I say so.'

'Yes, ma'am.' Jeff's eyes twinkled. He seemed to take pleasure in saying it and, to be honest, so did I. This time the words stroked me like a warm hand.

Very few commercials are read 'live' on radio any more – it's too dangerous. A squeaky chair or rattling script can ruin it, even if you don't flub your lines. Still, some clients liked the spontaneous flavour, and I knew I was good at it. With Jeff as an audience I was *great*.

He was rapt, enthralled. I felt his gaze as if it was a tangible heat source, the steady, bone-warming glow of a radiator. My eyes stole away from the script to savour him: his square-shouldered stance pulled his shirt tight across his chest, nipples raising the fabric like kernels of corn; the solid jut in his work pants wasn't a hard-on but a healthy animal readiness.

And he waited against the wall because I'd told him to. The idea was slick and wanton, and sent curls of excitement into my thighs.

'. . . So settle back and relax in the luxury of fine furniture from Hanson's. You deserve it.'

Even when I'd turned off the mike and punched in the next pre-recorded ad, Jeff waited, obediently still.

I finally laughed. 'At ease, soldier.'

'That was amazing.' The words were hushed with awe. 'You sound like smoke and steel.'

'Oh, it's a little genetics and a whole lot of training.'

He shook his head. 'Maybe for the others, but you're different. That ballsy voice is *you*. The first time I heard it, I thought, that's one hard, hot lady. It's a dream come true to meet you. I've waited so long.'

He'd waited? My skin prickled, thin fingers of uneasiness crawling over my bare shoulders.

'How ... did you get this job?'

'I applied for it.' He grinned. 'Three times.'

Revelation smacked me awake. 'Are you a star fucker, Jeff?'

His smirk spread wide. 'Not yet. But the night isn't over, is it?'

Alarm ran from my heart to my hands, burst painfully in my fingertips. A fan or a stalker? I was alone in the station with God-knew-what. My thoughts whirled: push the panic button – no! Get him out of here – no! Get yourself out of this booth ...

Then fear ignited into something else. *How dare he.*

'You punk. You snot-nosed son of a bitch! Who the hell do you think you are?' A burning wave pushed me to my feet. 'I get cheap come-ons ten times a night from celebrity sluts like you. Yet you march in here with a vacuum cleaner and expect to be something different? Did you think I'd fall at your feet?'

Surprise had wiped the insolence off his face. He took a step. 'Sherry, I –'

'Back against the wall!'

He obeyed abruptly, shoulders hitting the wood with a satisfying thump. I glared at him, my heart pounding. But damn – this commercial break was ending. I felt a spasm of deep, ingrained reflex: keep the show on schedule.

My finger flew up, an order, a threat. 'Stay.'

I dropped into my chair and took a breath. I flicked the mike. Three, two and . . .

'Welcome back, night people. I'm Sherry Sharone on CHQT. It's two thirty-four, a long way to dawn, but I have mellow favourites from yesterday and today to get you there. And, hey! Didn't get your tickets for the Amanda Marshall concert? Well, you and five friends . . .'

I slid into the contest promo, the words flowing in a professional purr. The rush of adrenaline was still galloping through my body but I was riding it now, and it veered off suddenly.

So he wants you, I told myself. What are you so upset about? It's not like he's one of those nuts on the phone. If you'd met in a bar you would have danced a jig out the door with him.

Jeff hadn't moved. He remained at attention between the shelves, lips parted, breathing lightly. And something extraordinary was happening. I watched in fascination as his fly swelled into a pronounced bulge. I'd just yelled at him and he was getting a hard-on? My clit pulsed in sweet surprise.

He had to be uncomfortable, yet he still didn't stir. There was something about that – his arousal, discomfort and obedience – that stroked me. It plumbed the deep, silent fantasies that had pooled in my empty hours alone with the microphone.

For a brief moment, common sense raised its yappy head. It didn't stand a chance.

If he was dangerous he would have done something

THE ALL NIGHT **69**

already, or threatened to. He had a chance to jump me in the hallway, when my back was turned. He's followed every order I've given – so far.

'. . . your choice for smooth radio, QT One-oh-three.'

Music up, mike off. For a moment there was only the low simpering of the love-struck singer.

'You were right, Jeff. I *do* own the night – or I own this one. And I don't like to be surprised by sudden moves from mouthy pick-up artists. But that doesn't mean I can't be impressed.'

His gaze crept over, hesitant, hopeful.

'Now, if you made a mistake you can walk out of this station. I'll see that you get a referral for your next job. Or – you can keep me company. Show me that you know how to behave with a hard, hot lady. You want to be a star fucker? Persuade me.'

I felt a thrilling tremor, the power of the spoken word. I'd never said that to anyone, not even in my fantasies, yet it rolled off my tongue as easily as my own call letters.

'Here's the rule: nothing interferes with my show. And no surprises, nothing that might *alarm* me. There are two magic buttons in this room, Jeff. One is a direct line to the cop shop – I don't even have to talk. They'll be here before you can get out the front door.'

'And the other one?'

'Use your imagination.'

He paused, then smiled as he began to unbutton his shirt. 'I have plenty of that, ma'am.'

I stared, mesmerised. With the buttons free, he simply shrugged the shirt off and it melted to the floor. His chest was breathtaking. Naked, he looked larger, his broad pectoral muscles stretching out in smooth, hard undulations, divided down the centre by a line of flat brown hair. It thickened on its way into his pants: a bristly, animal promise over his abdomen.

'Give me your belt.' The coolness of my voice astonished me. Where had those words come from?

The colour of his eyes deepened to hard hazelnut. He unhooked the buckle then pulled it out of the loops, a brown snake gleaming dully.

He faltered and I saw his predicament – how was he going to get it to me without throwing it? Suddenly he folded the belt into an elongated figure of eight, and clamped it between his teeth. It looped on either side of his face like a bow, and spread his mouth in a grimace: a bridle or a gag. The sight seared me. My pussy lips throbbed, wet and engorged, pushing against the cotton centre of my panties.

With the belt still in his mouth, Jeff slid down the wall, then scooted across the floor on his ass and hands, beneath the level of the window. He slipped under the control board, next to my bare legs.

It happened so swiftly I almost shrieked. Instead, I wheeled my chair back and glared down at him. He was crouched in the opening like an oversized dog in a kennel.

'What the hell are you doing?'

He offered the belt to me. 'I thought I could massage your feet.'

The folded leather was stiff, resilient in my grasp. I felt the wet spot where his tongue had touched and it sent an illicit tingle through me, as if he'd licked my hand.

'All right. As long as you're quiet.' I slipped my feet out of my sandals.

Jeff's hands were hot, strong and experienced. He rubbed slow, delicious circles around my ankles, drew long lines of pressure with his thumbs. Every digit was patiently caressed. Adored. Molten pleasure flowed through my legs like lava, straight into the waiting portal of my cunt.

The tart scent rose from under my loose summer skirt. I was sure he could smell me; I could smell myself. Leaning back in my chair, I watched him through heavy eyes, relished the big, half-naked body crouched at my feet. I felt like a sultana: powerful and decadent. My free foot rested on one of his thighs, and I slid it over to his crotch, letting the prodigious bulge fill the curve of my arch. Granite. I ached for it.

But this sultana still had a show to do. I forced myself upright to reach the microphone.

'Not a peep,' I ordered, and underscored the command with light but distinct pressure on his crotch, the way you accelerate a car over a rise. I heard a low, ragged breath beneath the control board – pain or pleasure? My pussy swam. It was all pleasure to me.

Mike on. Music fade. 'Ooh, that lady's voice is something else, isn't it? Melissa Etheridge, and before that . . .'

Movement beneath the desk: I felt Jeff lift my foot higher. Before I could register surprise, wet heat sizzled in a white line up my leg. My God, he was sucking my toes! For a second I was speechless, the most dreaded offence: dead air. Then my survival instinct kicked in and I heard my own voice as if from a distance, a liquid growl.

'. . . smooth favourites to sail you away – QT One-oh-three.'

Jeff began to lick his way up the inside of my left leg.

I leaned back and pushed my ass to the front of the chair, hiking my skirt high over my thighs. Jeff's free hand teased me through my panties, thick fingers stroking the soaked fabric. When I stretched the cotton panel over to one side, the heat of my sex must have hit him like a furnace. Jeff moaned in his throat and moved up eagerly, straining to reach me with his mouth, his head squeezed into the tight opening between my legs and the top of the control board. But I couldn't move back to give him room – we would have been in full view of the window. His tongue just managed to reach me and darted at my sex in dainty, maddening little flickers, a snake tasting the air.

Oh, God, I had to ride this man.

I pushed his face away. His brown eyes were ethereal; his exquisite mouth smeared.

'Yes, Sherry?'

'Go to the women's washroom and wait on the couch. Be ready. We won't have much time.'

About twelve minutes, actually. I could programme the computer to automatically play four songs in a row, no more. It was the station's way of making sure none of us slipped out for a beer.

Jeff left the control room in a bent-over crouch, a contortion that sent a welt of delight through me. I programed the queue of songs one-handed, pressing my sex with the other. It was another insipid line-up dictated by my Play List, but I could have fucked that man to the soundtrack of *Mary Poppins*.

I rummaged in my purse for a condom, then, as a last thought, I grabbed Jeff's abandoned shirt – he'd need it later. A laminated card fell from the pocket and I bent to retrieve it. It was his cleaning company photo-ID tag: Carl Weaver.

My eyes zigzagged between the photo and the name. Why the hell hadn't he given me his right one? Then revelation thumped me in the chest. Carl! It was the same Romeo who phoned me all the time on the request line, I was sure of it. But why hadn't I recognised his voice?

Because I'd been too busy ogling his body. He'd known I would, that sneaky, lying son of a bitch!

He's also hot, Sherry. He almost set your panties on fire. You want him – why the hell are you so upset?

Because the prick tried to put one over on me. I remembered his flattery in the hallway: Sherry Sharone was nobody's fool.

Damn right. The Princess of Pop kicked off the set and I charged out of the control room – I had eleven minutes, twenty-four seconds. I was halfway down the hall before I realised I still had his belt, folded over in my clenched hand.

The ladies' room was feminine but spare: in addition to the sinks and stalls there were cheap silk flowers, a full-length mirror and a red faux-leather couch. He was sitting on it in his underwear, but when I opened the door he got to his feet, a painful rip of hot skin separating from vinyl.

Good. Suffer a little, I thought.

Then my gaze dropped; I couldn't help it. His underwear was a cross between briefs and boxers, clingy, white, thigh-hugging shorts that pushed out in a thick, delectable swell. *Cock*. The knowledge seared me, an electric V surged beneath by navel. I almost swayed, but caught myself.

'Do you think you're clever?' I demanded.

If he'd planned to sweep me into his arms, he changed his mind. 'Sherry . . .?'

'Answer me! Do you think you're a smart ass, *Carl*?'

Now he knew. He assessed me for a moment; his eyes touched on the belt. Then he fell into a new stance, feet spaced in line with his shoulders, hands clasped dutifully behind his back. He stared over my shoulder at the far wall, the distant, respectful gaze of a private getting court-martialled.

'No, ma'am. I was just willing to do anything to meet you.'

His obedient military pose was intoxicating. I tried to shake it off. 'Did you think I was stupid, that I wouldn't find out?'

'No, ma'am, I assumed you would.'

'Then why? What the hell did you expect me to do?'

The words were low, thick, a hungry secret. 'Punish me, ma'am. Good and hard.'

The wallop of desire made me drunk. The room seemed to waver with sex. Surreal. Over the loudspeaker, the Princess was winding down to a syrupy finish; Bette Midler's oldie was up next. Because of the mirror I could see both Carl's front and back, his hands clenched over his white ass and the hard-on that threatened to break through his fly. My whole body simmered with immanent heat, cunt and heart throbbing in rhythm.

'Then pull off your shorts and show me how you want it.'

He was breathing rapidly through parted lips, eyes half-closed in a dream. But the rest of him moved with deft precision. When he flipped down his underwear, his cock bobbed, a meaty shock of male colour. His nest of dark, wild hair flattened into an intricate swirl on its way down his athletic legs. In that girlie room he looked like a beast.

But a well-trained one. Carl turned to the stalls and reached above his head, gripped the metal beam over a door. He shifted to find his footing, bracing himself. The bridge of naked skin was an alluring shock against the grey metal backdrop, his vulnerability stretched out and waiting for me.

I'd never done this – and yet I had. Hand between my legs, pictures flashing against my eyelids. Or mouth to the microphone, swept away in the throaty stream of my own voice while my mind skimmed across a vast, bottomless sea.

I wrapped one end of the belt around my hand, buckle in my palm. Bette was crooning above us, her voice like polished brass.

'*It must have been cold there in my shadow...*'

Crack! The sound reverberated through the bathroom, sharper and wetter than it really was. God, I loved an echo. Crack! The contact of the leather on his skin went through my whole body; my pussy clutched hungrily.

'*...I could fly higher than an eagle...*'

Pink stripes were rising on his ass and legs. I felt the glow radiating from my own centre, as if I was beaming the colour onto him. A beacon.

'Harder, Sherry. I can take it.'

Crack! Carl's skin gleamed; the dark hair up the cleft of his buttocks was flattened by sweat. Every blow forced a grunt from him now, a guttural breath of endurance. I drank the sound like champagne.

When I glanced at the mirror I caught a sliver of raw wickedness: the brown leather snake licking at Carl's hard, muscle-knotted body and the ruddy cock that leaped beneath. Behind him my own curvy female form was swaying in a dance, skirt swinging, heavy breasts in a tube top shuddering along with the lash.

I knew if I touched myself I would come.

'... *thank God for you, the wind beneath my wings.*'

Bette's big finish. Two songs left, I had just over six minutes. 'All right. That's enough.'

Carl's arms dropped from his handhold. He turned, panting, eyes a liquid plea. A gleaming dribble leaked from the swollen mushroom head of his cock. I wondered if a whipping alone could make him shoot.

Well, we weren't going to find out tonight. I tossed him the condom packet, then reached under my skirt to yank off my panties.

'Let's go, boy.'

I let him take me from on top. I welcomed his sweaty weight, and was surprised by the care he took in entering me; I truly felt the rigid, luxuriant shape of his cock, every firm curve as he opened me. My breath escaped in a long rasp of fulfilment. I was finally plugged into the Earth's current and yet I was that power, too. It flowed from me.

Carl began to buck, the ancient, lawless drive of thunder. He burned me against the carpet with instinctive, animal thrusts. I loved the sensation, pushed up to meet it, yet I revelled in the look of him: face contorted, eyes squeezed shut, a low desperate song rising up from his balls. I dug my heels into the small of his back to spur him and he twisted with a fresh moan, his pleasure shot through by the renewed stings. I was certain I could feel the heat of his stripes on my ankles.

It ignited me. In my mind's eye I saw it all again: his mouth spread by the folded leather, his muscular nakedness clinging to the beam. I felt the shock of contact that sizzled into my body through the belt. Lightning rod.

Bright, twitching loveliness. My pussy muscles squeezed and released, to clutch again in sweetness. Ecstasy sparkled on my surface, sunlight on waves, but far below I felt the movement of stronger currents, water bending.

'Coming!' Carl barked. I had the gratification of watching him from a point of silky serenity, riding his pulses while I still rode my own, enjoying him writhe and smooth out again, gasping. It stirred me with a nameless satisfaction. Triumph.

We gazed at each other for a moment, hearts thumping. Then the silence drove into me like a needle: dead air.

'Get off, get off!'

Can you float at a run? I hurried down the hall, tugging up my skirt, air cooling my sweat-sticky skin. My whole body was heavy with ebbing bliss, but my mind sprinted. How long had we been off the air – twenty seconds, thirty? I burst into the control room.

'Woo ... Andre Bocelli on QT One-hundred-and-three. That man's so hot I actually melted.'

Somehow I kept going, a languorous chatter that rose from a secret place, my own creamy centre. My voice was caramel. I knew I'd be in shit over the blank air, and I didn't care. They wanted me to glide? Hell, I was soaring.

And thinking. In my mind's eye I saw Carl getting dressed down the hall, imagined him pulling up his shorts over the pink stripes on his backside. I wondered how long the colour would last and felt a strange gust, both hard and tender. Possessive.

I glanced out of the window at the familiar city lights, still spread like a scattering of stars. I didn't need to gather them all in my hands. It was enough to hold just the one.

My impulse was naughty, definitely *not* on my Play List, but I was in trouble already. And I wanted to give him something. The All Night was no longer a shift, it had become an adventure.

'We'll start off our next set with a song for a very special guy. Carl, this one's for you, some old gold from John Mellencamp.'

I cranked my monitor. The brazen, ballsy guitar seemed to shake the whole sleepy building and seconds later the control room door opened. My toy soldier was grinning from ear to ear.

I'd chosen, of course, 'Hurts So Good'.

Marks in the Mirror
Francesca Brouillard

It was ten days before the marks disappeared completely but I kept checking long after that, twisting
round awkwardly in front of the bathroom mirror.
Those shocking pink stripes held a disturbing fascination. Oddly I felt quite disappointed when they'd
gone; there was almost a sense of loss.

That first time he did it to me the overriding sensation
was shock. Pure shock. I felt panic and fear as well,
but shock was the main thing. Then the inevitable
pain. A smarting, burning, humiliating pain. Anger
came later, sizzling orange and confused, bubbling
with indignation and spiced with shame.

Afterwards, when finally I looked at him, I was
surprised to find his face strangely devoid of emotion.
It was not twisted or flushed from some sadistic
pleasure. Just nothing.

That same evening as we'd sat opposite each other
over supper, a slanting sun turning stray crumbs to
gold, he'd behaved as if nothing had happened.
Chewing on the remains of a baguette and the
inevitable goat cheese, he'd talked about his child-
hood and hot summers spent there in the Pyrenees,
minding the goats with his father.

The previous day he could have captivated me with his stories and I would have asked about his current life in Paris but right then, *that* evening, I was too consumed with anger to even hear his words. The humiliating scene from the morning replayed itself in my head till the very air around me vibrated with tension. I picked at my food distractedly and wriggled; sitting was painful.

As if suddenly aware of my discomfort he broke off his story and looked at me.

'Eva . . .' Despite his excellent English he had not been able to pronounce Eve, so he'd taken to calling me Eva, which his French accent made rather exotic.

'Eva, you have a problem with your seat, I think. Would you prefer to take a cushion?'

Was that a smile twitching at the corner of his mouth? I blushed furiously and had a sudden violent urge to hurl the pitcher of wine over him. I stopped myself; I wasn't going to give him the satisfaction of seeing my rage.

I began to wish that Angelline, whose company I'd rather resented the previous day, was still there. Ineffectually adolescent though she was, another presence would have prevented anything happening.

Back here in my office those few weeks on the farm, and in particular the days spent on the mountain, seem so remote as to be unreal. Memories of the rank overpowering smell of goats, hot afternoons on the hillside and the sour odour of cheese wafting up through the floorboards seem to belong to another lifetime. I could almost believe it had never existed.

Almost. But for the marks in the mirror – which

have finally gone – and a dark, uneasy feeling, which won't.

As I dash between board meetings and conferences in an expensive cloud of perfume, juggling accounts, investment options and a team of financial experts, I wonder how that slow pace of life and its dull routines had ever appealed to me.

I press the buzzer on my desk. 'Maureen, can you send Jacob through and tell him to bring the figures for October.'

I feel slightly irked at having to deal with Jacob today. I suspect he's been slacking while I've been away and needs bringing back in line. It's always difficult in management, keeping people up to speed. Some of my team, generally the university recruits, think I'm pushy and ruthless, but they're on top money so I expect top performance. Maureen let slip that certain ones amongst them refer to me as the Rottweiler. I took a private pleasure in that.

'Ah, Jacob. Take a seat.'

I was wrong earlier when I said Louis' expression was devoid of emotion after that first incident. I just wasn't able to see the complexity of his motives then.

Although the Caribbean is usually more my line, this year I'd decided to go and stay with my cousin and her family in France. The decision was prompted by Naomi, my regular holiday mate, dumping me for her new bloke and my having no one else to go with.

I suppose I'm what some people would call a workaholic. I love the power and responsibility that come with my job; the decision-making, the control, the team of people working for me – it all gives me a buzz and sense of importance. Inevitably, though, I don't have much time or energy for a social life, nor a great deal of opportunity to meet people. Men, I mean. Of course I'm surrounded by them at work, as Naomi constantly points out, and some of them are attractive enough, but they're always the wrong sort; those on my managerial scale are inevitably in their fifties while the younger ones have not yet made the grade. It may sound arrogant, but I couldn't envisage a relationship with a man lower down the hierarchy. It's a matter of status.

Anyway, it was my lack of holiday companion that initially made me think of going to France. My cousin Holly and her French husband have been renovating their farm in the Pyrenees for what feels like decades, and they've recently converted a barn into gîtes and gone over to organic farming. They have a flock of goats and sheep and specialise in producing cheese using traditional methods. I know I'm welcome there − as Holly says, an extra pair of hands is always useful − and the prospect of sun, mountains and fresh air presented an attractive alternative to the dusty bustle of London in summer.

Michel, Holly's husband, met me at the airport in Perpignon. On the drive back we chatted about family, business, and what was happening on the farm; they had two families in the gîtes and a teenager, Angelline, staying with them over the holidays. In addition there were a couple of local guys helping with the animals and cheese-making. One I'd met previously but the other, Louis, now lived in Paris and was just back for the summer.

When I was introduced to him later at dinner he

nodded at me curtly and caught my eye for just long enough to make me feel I'd been weighed up and found lacking. This perfunctory dismissal irritated me, and I would have had nothing more to do with him had it not been for a certain dangerous allure beneath that supercilious exterior.

I spent the first week hanging around the farm and chatting with Holly. Our afternoons would be spent preparing the evening meal, which formed the focal point of the day. Sometimes we were joined by the families from the gîtes or neighbours, but it was always a large and noisy, sociable occasion. These were the only times I saw Louis, and despite a few attempts at conversation, I always felt tense around him and experienced a disconcerting fluttering in my belly.

When Holly asked me during my second week if I'd like to spend a few days in the hut on the mountain I was delighted. I remembered it as a stone ruin sheltering below a crag, but it had been repaired since my last visit, to enable someone to stay with the goats over summer. Louis would be relieving the current shepherd, and Angelline had asked if she could go along.

I was both pleased and disappointed with this arrangement. The whole goats and mountains and back-to-nature thing had a very romantic appeal; it was the stuff fantasies are made of. However, the combination of an adolescent chaperone and a man about whom I felt ambivalent detracted somewhat from this idyll.

After a couple of days at the hut Angelline started her period and wanted to go back down to the farm, a feeling I could sympathise with given our rustic sanitary conditions. I rather welcomed this development at the time, thinking that a few days alone with Louis might ease the awkwardness between us and even lead to something more promising. What naivety! Away from the sociable environment of the farm he barely bothered responding to my conversational overtures, and my few attempts at charming him with a nice meal or compliments were completely ignored. Even when I offered to help with the milking he showed little grace, just issuing curt instructions and criticising my clumsiness.

Perversely, though perhaps predictably, the more he ignored me the more I felt attracted to him. I began having erotic dreams that lingered long after waking. Dreams that took me to the edge of a precipice and left me poised there on the verge of orgasm. Dreams from which I woke to find myself lying in a sweat, my hand between my legs. Dreams that filtered through the thin dividing wall that separated me from his sleeping body and tortured me with their elusive desire.

It was these dreams, surely, and the fractured sleepless nights, that drove me to the shameful act that triggered that first 'incident'. How else could I account for finding myself in the cold pink of dawn, crouching behind a tree, spying on him? I'd slipped out of the hut a few minutes after I heard him leave, pulling a jumper over my pyjamas and making straight for the wooded crag above the stream. From there I knew I'd be able to see the small pool we used for bathing.

From my hidden vantage point I heard the

scrunching of pebbles under his boots as he came into view. At the water's edge, he stooped to take off his shoes and socks then tugged his sweater over his head, in that way men do, from the neck. His body was lean and functional-looking; you could see the sharp curves of muscle carved by work rather than work-outs.

His hands dropped to his belt. I swallowed and ran my tongue over my cracked lips. Surely he could hear my heart thumping? He slid his pants down, stepped out of them and waded into the pool. The pale buttocks tensed and hollowed as the water crept icily up his thighs, and I could almost feel the goose pimples on my own body. He bent over and splashed water over his head and chest. When he stood again I could clearly see the black stripe of hair that ran down his belly and fanned out above his penis. Behind my own pubic bone a muscle tautened. If I'd hoped to find vulnerability in his nakedness then I was to be disappointed; as I watched him wash, his brisk, unselfconscious movements evoked the unpredictable power of a stallion.

I left as he was dressing.

As I reached a rocky outcrop above the hut I found myself suddenly face to face with Louis. He was sitting nonchalantly on a boulder beside the path. Waiting. My mouth went dry.

'Ah, Eva!'

I tried a smile and wondered whether to feign innocence. I didn't get the chance. He stood as I approached, grabbed me by the arm and shoved me up against the rock. There wasn't even time to struggle. He twisted me round and forced me over till I was face down on the rock. I felt the hard coldness against my chest and an edge grazed my hips through my pyjamas. When I tried to raise my head he pushed me down roughly.

Did I scream or fight back? I don't know. I remember being aware of sharp pebbles digging into my breast and the hollow, empty-belly feeling of shock. Then terror rose like a suffocating balloon in my throat, threatening to choke me. What was he going to do? Please don't let him rape me! That was my first thought. Oh please, God, don't let him do that! I tried to think of things to say. Should I plead? Apologise?

I felt his hand brush my bottom and pull up my sweater. Was he going to bugger me? No, I would die! It was unthinkable.

That's when I felt the first blow. I screamed, though it was more from shock than anything else; he'd slapped me across the backside as if I were a naughty child! Perhaps that was it; it was just a joke. I was being smacked in punishment for spying on him. He was going to teach me a lesson. Perhaps it was even his idea of a come-on.

The second and third slaps swiftly dispelled that notion, scalding my buttocks with glowing humiliation. If this was a joke then he was far too heavy-handed. This hurt! Seriously. The next slap left my backside burning as if a hot iron had been put to my flesh. I was crying now, loud gulping sobs broken by yells with each slap. Any resistance I might have shown dissolved under his punitive palm.

There were, I think, no more than half a dozen spanks on that first occasion, yet they were enough to keep me spread helpless over the rock for several minutes after he'd stopped.

When finally I stood up, dishevelled and tear-stained, I was too embarrassed to look at him. I hated him. I hated him for witnessing me in this state; for seeing my shame, my indignity, my humiliation. Perhaps I hated him more for this, oddly enough, than for the ordeal he'd just put me through.

And when I did eventually look at him ... I saw nothing.

That night I lay for a long time debating what I should do. I could hardly pretend nothing had happened. Maybe I should confront him and have it out. It would be too embarrassing to tell Holly and Michel. I could just pack my bags and leave, but that would be cowardly. Besides, he'd think he'd got the better of me.

Eventually I drifted off into a restless sleep where lustful hands overpowered me, pinned me down, and pleasured me in unimaginable ways. Hot mouths licked me, sucked me, pressed against my sex and nibbled me. Although I couldn't see them in my dream I knew they were his hands, his mouth.

When I woke I was sticky between the thighs. I didn't pack my bags.

I'd thought I'd feel an overwhelming relief to get back to the farm and Holly and normality, but somehow it was an anticlimax; everything felt rather bland and mundane. As before I only saw Louis at meals, where he was polite but distant, and this in a peculiar way irritated me. It was as if he was pretending that nothing had happened. At the same time I was angry with myself for colluding with him. By saying and doing nothing I was permitting the 'incident' to become our secret, as if I'd consented to it.

Holly could sense that I was on edge at the farm, and asked if I wanted to spend my last week at the hut. I knew Michel was doing a stint on the mountain and I reckoned a few days of his easy-going good humour would restore my equilibrium. I was beginning to relax after a couple of days of his company when Louis appeared. He'd come to relieve Michel who was, apparently, needed on the farm.

Was this a pretext? Had Louis volunteered to relieve Michel because he knew I was up there? There was no way of finding out. My stomach had leaped with excitement at the sight of him, but the feeling was quickly soured by anger and a dark, creeping dread that tiptoed close to fear. I could have gone down, of course. But maybe by then I couldn't.

The following afternoon, Louis startled me as I was washing up. I'd been nervy since he'd arrived, and his very presence made me clumsy and awkward, so it was no surprise, when he burst through the door unexpectedly, that I dropped a plate. It smashed around my feet with a sickening ring, and I froze.

Everything after seemed to happen in slow motion. Louis put down his bag, walked over to me and bent to pick up the broken pieces. I stood there, unable to respond, unable even to think. He placed the pieces in the sink then took me by the arm. My heart banged against my ribs and my legs became rubbery.

I could have resisted, I suppose, or run away, but I didn't. I allowed myself to be led to the table and, when he instructed me to lean over, I obeyed. As his hand pressed down between my shoulder blades, flattening me against the tabletop, I felt a jolt of anticipation shoot up my thighs and into my sex.

My loose cotton skirt gave scant protection against his ruthless hand. Though I managed to suppress my cries initially, the repeated slaps soon had me crying aloud as each muffled thwack branded my backside with the imprint of his palm. It seemed to go on endlessly, the sound of his hand and the sharp shock of pain followed by the deep purple throbbing of my bruised flesh. Hot tears burned streaks of shame down my face and formed undignified puddles on the table.

I couldn't bear to face him when he stopped – I felt too humiliated – but he took hold of my chin and tilted my head till I was forced to look at him. His expression was disturbing. It made me feel naked and vulnerable, as if he had some hold over me. I looked away quickly.

I was wrong earlier when I said I couldn't see the complexity of his motives in his face. It was that I was scared by what I saw.

The next few days passed without incident. Louis was out most of the time with the animals, and I wandered over the hills or lay reading by the stream. During the evenings we co-existed uneasily in an atmosphere of sexual tension and stilted conversation. Neither of us made any allusion to the spanking.

When my last day arrived I felt both relief and a strange disappointment, as if something hadn't quite lived up to my expectations. Louis and I were awkward around each other, trying to maintain a physical distance that the hut didn't really permit. It made me stupid and clumsy, so that I bumped into things and dropped my clothes as I packed. Inevitably disaster ensued. I knocked a jug of milk with my elbow and sent it splashing into the sink. A silly accident that didn't really matter, but I knew what would follow.

I looked at Louis. I almost wanted something to happen; the tension between us, like the air before a thunderstorm, had grown electric. He held my gaze and my skin tingled. Slowly, without taking his eyes from mine, he lowered his hands to his waist and began to unbuckle his belt. My heart quickened. He pulled the belt from his trousers and ran it thoughtfully through his hands as if testing its suppleness, then nodded towards the table.

'Bend over, Eva.'

My mouth was dry and I noticed my hands were trembling as I placed them on the table under my cheek.

'Pull your jeans down.' His voice was low, controlled. I made to stand up to undo my jeans but he pushed me back down, forcing me to struggle awkwardly with the zip while my hips were pressed up against the table. I managed to wriggle them down over my backside then felt him tug them further down. My briefs began to creep up between my buttocks, a trivial detail under the circumstances, yet something about the intimacy of it heightened my sense of vulnerability.

I tensed as the leather cut the air with a whistle and cracked sharply on my flesh. There was a timeless pause, then a searing stripe of agony painted the world red and emptied my lungs in a gasp. My whole body shook with the shock, and I would have collapsed had I not been laid out on the table. I tried to raise myself to protest, but felt his fingertips lightly on my back. Obeying his unspoken command I submitted and gripped the edge of the table. Again the cruel crack of leather as another lash drew a weal across my backside and a scream from my throat. Please, no more! No more! I bit my lip to keep the words inside and tasted the hot saltiness of blood mixing with my tears. I sensed him raising his arm again, and dug my nails into the table. An eternity passed. Had he changed his mind? Had he decided it was enough? I breathed out cautiously. Then it fell. Cruel. Scorching. A savage arc across the other two lashes, leaving me too exhausted to sob. I was unable to move for a long time. Finally he helped me stand and made me a coffee with brandy.

When eventually I reached home after an agonising journey, I took a long bath and examined myself in the mirror. My backside was scored with three raised red weals. It was ten days before they finally disappeared.

It was such a relief to get back to work. The huge backlog of accounts kept me late in the office and exhausted enough to sleep soundly all night. Lunchtimes – when I took them – I spent obsessively in the gym trying to shed the weight I'd put on from all that goat cheese. Everything fell so neatly back into its time-allotted slot there was no available space for my mind to consider the disturbing events that had taken place, or for my emotions to run riot with my body.

The buzzer on my desk goes.

'Someone to see you, Eve. Says it's personal. Are you busy?'

'Yeah, but send them through anyway, Maureen. I'll deal with it.' It would probably be one of the juniors needing leave for a grandmother's funeral or something.

I'm checking a summary of accounts so I don't look up when the door opens – I'm also slightly annoyed they haven't knocked.

'Hello, Eva.'

My body responds to his voice before my brain has even processed the information. There is a tightening in my groin and my stomach somersaults. My pen falls to the floor. I start to rise but he stays by the door and I am left in an awkward crouched position behind my desk, unsure whether to go and greet him or sit back down.

My mind searches desperately for an appropriate response. I must say something but nothing seems suitable. I don't even know whether or not I'm pleased to see him. In the end I just come out with a rather strangled 'Louis!'

He leans back against the door and looks at me with the sort of half smile that shows he is fully aware of having the advantage. It's too late to go over and embrace him, the moment has passed, and my hands are trembling too much to extend in a handshake. I must take charge of the situation. This is my office, for god's sake – he can't just come in here and set the rules! Not that he has actually done anything, but my thoughts have become jumbled and incoherent. And all the time he is just watching me. I try a smile.

'So what brings you here, Louis?' It sounds so artificial and smug I feel myself blush.

'I've come to see *you*, Eva.' His arms are folded across his chest and he looks quite relaxed. Inside my blouse I have broken out in a sweat, yet there are goose pimples down my arms and breasts. I have a sudden panic that my nipples are visible and giving off all the wrong messages, so I cross my arms and lean forwards on my desk. Take charge, Eve. Say something.

'Are you over here on business, then?' What a stupid question.

'No. I'm here to see you.'

'You mean you've come specially? All the way from the farm?'

'I'm back in Paris now. For work. But yes, I've come to see you.'

My heart thumps inside my ribs and I'm not sure if it's panic or something more frightening. Get a grip! He has a small smile on his lips but I don't think he's mocking me. I attempt a light-hearted laugh but it sounds hysterical, like a woman on the edge.

'I've come to see if you're happy now you're back in England.'

'Of course I'm happy. I've a great job, a nice home...' It comes out too fast, too gushing. Whoa, Eve, stop trying so hard. Slow down. I clear my throat, take a breath.

'I've every reason to be happy, haven't I?'

His face doesn't alter – still that little smile – but

he looks at me steadily, as you might look at a child you were waiting for to admit the truth.

'I felt that perhaps you had come to France to get away from something.' His voice is soft and even, his accent seductive. 'Or maybe to find something.' The question mark is in the raised eyebrow, the slight tilt of his head inviting confession.

I have a sudden desire to touch him, to run my fingers along his cheek, to press myself against him.

'No, I'm perfectly content with my life, thank you.' My voice is all prim and uptight. I hate myself.

'*Eh bien*, I shall say goodbye, Eva. It seems I have misread the situation.' And he turns to open the door.

What have I done wrong? Which was the wrong answer? I feel like I've been given a test, which I failed, and now he's leaving. No second chance.

'Wait!' There's desperation in my voice. He looks round at me but doesn't move.

'Louis . . .' I must say something to detain him. A little longer at least. 'Please . . . just come in . . . don't go yet.' He shuts the door, leans back and waits. I can't think what to say. Everything seems either too trivial or too dangerous. I play for time.

'Have you seriously come just to see me?' I try to make my voice light and casual. He doesn't answer but continues looking at me. Waiting. I glance down at my hands and notice they are tugging at the hem of my shirt.

'I . . . Why are you bothered whether I'm happy or not?' I must keep talking to keep him here. Yet why? I'd thought when the marks went, those last signs of his hold over me, I'd be able to forget him – that I'd *want* to forget him – yet here I am making a fool of myself in an attempt to stop him leaving. Still he says nothing.

'I'm, er ... glad you are here, anyway.' Do I sound trite and insincere?

'Eva, why do you have such a problem talking to me? Don't you know what I want?' He frowns at me and butterflies create havoc in my belly. 'Don't you know what *you* want?'

I feel as if my body desires one thing while my common sense tells me something else entirely. I drop my head into my hands. Don't make me think about dangerous things. Leave me to my busy, important life. I don't want complications. I want to stay safe and in control.

'You need me, Eva.'

I look up, shocked. Perhaps I've misheard. But he holds my gaze, challenging me to deny it. Suddenly the messy confusion of my emotions focuses into one angry, clear thought – the bloody audacity of the man! The sheer pigheaded cheek of him, to imagine that I, with my prestigious job and respectable salary, should need him: I am livid.

'Need you! Why on earth should I need a ...' I search furiously for a suitably cutting insult. 'A pervert!'

He tilts his head slightly. 'Ah, so that's what you call it in English.' His voice is still soft and quiet but I sense an air of danger behind it. I feel myself redden. He strides up to the desk and leans over me.

'So you think I have strange desires? Maybe you think I like to humiliate women. To punish them, eh? Is this how you see me then, Eva?' There is an impatience to his voice now, a passion, and I'm nervous. My eyes shift along the desk to the buzzer.

'Well, Eva, is this the sort of man you think I am?' Suddenly his hand is under my chin, tipping my head back till I'm forced to look at him. A tremor runs through my body at the contact, but I'm not sure whether it's due to fear or lust. He holds my eyes in his till I shake my head. I know it was an unfair accusation, but in some ways it was preferable to the alternatives – the things I can't admit.

I lied earlier when I said I was scared by the motives I saw in his face. I was scared by what they showed me about myself. Scared to discover I had a perverse side to me. Scared too that someone else could see it.

He lets go of my chin but remains leaning forwards over me.

'Have you never asked yourself why you let me do that to you? You could have stopped me. You could have told someone. You could have packed your bags and left. But you didn't. Why not, Eva, why not?'

I have no answer. I can't even formulate a reason to myself. Perhaps I don't dare. He stands up abruptly and walks back to the door. I have a sudden panic that he might just walk out on me. Go. Forever. I open my mouth but at the door he stops. Then he leans back against the wall, folds his arms and waits. There is a long silence. I realise I'm terrified he'll leave now. It is as if he's lifted the lid off a deep, deep well and left me perched on the edge.

When he finally speaks his voice is hard.

'Take your shirt off.'

The command catches me off guard.

'Take your shirt off, Eva!'

When I don't respond he lowers his hands to his belt. No! Not here. My hand flies to the buzzer on my desk in alarm. He can't do that to me here, in my own office.

'Maureen?'

He pauses, holding me in his gaze, and for a moment time is suspended; then, without taking his eyes from mine, he begins to unbuckle his belt. I swallow. I desperately need to assert myself. This is *my* domain, where *I* should be in control.

'Eve? Did you call me?'

Yet inside me is another equally compelling force. A dark, unspeakable desire I can't admit to. Neither of us moves.

'Eve, is everything all right?'

Slowly he continues undoing his belt and pulls it from round his waist. A pulse throbs between my legs and I press my thighs together.

'Eve! Is anything the matter?'

'Sorry, Maureen. No, everything's fine. I just want you to divert my calls and . . . and . . .' He is running the belt slowly, calculatedly through his hands. 'And, Maureen, could you see that I'm not disturbed. Thanks.'

He folds his arms and lets the belt dangle from one hand.

'Take it off, Eva.'

Slowly I begin unbuttoning my top. I slip it off my shoulders and lay it on the desk.

'Now the bra.'

I'm suddenly shy. Although he's seen me stripped of my dignity he's never seen me undressed before.

'Stand up!'

I push my chair back and rise.

'Take off your bra.'

I reach behind me, unhook it and, after a pause, let it fall forwards, freeing my breasts. They feel swollen, conspicuous. I feel his eyes on them and look away, embarrassed. As he approaches me I want to cross my arms over my chest but I don't dare.

'Lean over the desk.'

I obey.

'Pull up your skirt. All the way. Now remove your pants.'

I do as he says, struggling to get my underwear over the spiked heels as I rest forwards on my chin and breasts. His hand is on my back, but lightly, not pinning me down; he knows he doesn't need to.

The anticipation sends a thrill through my body that makes me shudder involuntarily, and I'm afraid he will construe it as a tremor of fear or, worse, desire. Though I have to admit it, my dread of the lash is laced with an excitement I know is sexual.

I hear the whistle of leather then the harsh crack of contact that turns my world red. I stifle a cry. Louis leans forwards, takes my shirt and shoves it in my mouth. The second lash lands directly over the first, and I choke a humiliated cry into my shirt. I bite down hard as I hear him raise the belt and bring it down again. It licks round the crease of my buttocks with a force that ricochets round every nerve ending in my body. I know I can't take any more; he will have me begging to stop if he raises the belt once more. But already I can feel the blood rushing between my legs; the gooiness inside, even as my eyes blink back the tears.

As the throbbing radiates out in pulsing waves I

picture the raised welts he will have painted on me, the secret signature of his power. I will relish them later in the mirror, those angry red imprints that confirm his control over me. I wonder how long they will last.

My face is wet with tears when he stops. He steps back then moves my chair away from the desk and into the centre of the room.

'Sit down but keep your skirt up.' I lower myself gently into the seat, biting my lip to avoid crying out in pain. The wood is cold against my burning backside. Soothing.

'Open your legs. Wider!' He is leaning against my desk, the belt beside him. His voice becomes softer now, almost husky. 'Now touch yourself.'

I try to imagine how I must appear to him, blotchy-faced, dishevelled and naked but for my heels and the skirt bunched around my waist. My widespread legs and bare breasts, heavy with the extra pounds I've put on recently, must make me look tarty and brazen. I put my hand to my pubes and rub gently. His eyes follow my movements. Under my fingertips I feel my clitoris respond.

'Inside, Eva. Push your fingers up.'

I tilt my hips back and press my fingers into the warm silkiness of my slit.

'No − inside, properly. I want to see you fuck yourself.' The vulgar phrase sounds funny with his accent, somehow less aggressive. I push my fingers deeper, and they slide in easily. I am wetter than I thought. He strides over and I feel his hand grab my wrist. With something almost like tenderness, he raises it to his face and puts my fingers in his mouth, one by one. His tongue curls around each one in turn. I begin to melt. Suddenly, almost roughly, he takes my hand from his lips and pulls me to my feet.

'Put your hands against the wall,' he commands.

He pushes me so I am facing the wall, and makes me lean forwards on outstretched arms. Then, thrusting his knee between my legs, he kicks my feet outwards till I am splayed apart. I have barely found my balance when I feel his hand tighten on the back of my neck as the hard end of his cock shoves into me. There is a moment of exquisite pleasure as I feel myself forced open and entered, then a sharp pain as his pelvis slaps against the raw flesh of my buttocks. I cry out. The grip on my neck tightens and he pushes himself yet further into me.

I tilt my hips, offering myself up. The pain heightens the thrill of being penetrated, and desire envelops me in concentric circles of pleasure and pain as I submit to him. Finally I am able to succumb to that dark, inner self that wants to be overpowered, dominated, controlled. I groan.

He pulls out slightly and I feel my backside throbbing.

'Is this what you wanted, Eva?' His voice is a whisper, almost a hiss. I don't reply. He slaps me sharply on the side of my buttock.

'Is it, Eva? Isn't this what you wanted all along, for me to fuck you?'

I nod.

'But you need something else as well, don't you, Eva?' His voice is silky now, seductive, and he slides his cock easily back into me as he talks. 'You need to feel my power over you. *Ma puissance.* I must first become your master and teach you to obey.' He begins to move slowly in and out of me, making me gasp when he presses against my tender flesh.

'You are like the animal that needs to be disciplined before it can be rewarded.' As his movements become faster, deeper, I feel my own body responding. 'Like a wild creature that must be broken and dominated before it can be tamed.'

He reaches up and starts squeezing my breasts. The tension that has been gripping my body for weeks is suddenly concentrated in the muscles that suck his penis into my dark wetness. My hips thrust against him, embracing the delicious pain of contact. He pinches my nipples and I sense him beginning to swell inside me. Suddenly a dam inside me bursts, tearing a scream from my throat. I feel his teeth bite into my shoulder, then I explode as he floods me with his juices.

The mirror will be criss-crossed with the red welts and teeth marks of my lover tonight. Perhaps this time they won't fade.

I was wrong when I said I was scared by what I saw in his face and what it showed me about myself. What scared me was seeing that he knew, right from the start, what I was like. He knew exactly what I needed, what I desired, what he had to do.

Gone Shopping A. D. R. Forte

Usually, I make a point of disliking the distracted cellphone users. The drivers going ten miles under the speed limit, the idiots arguing in the middle of the grocery store aisle with their spouse or kid or pool contractor, blissfully blocking the tomato sauce from those of us who actually want to get our shopping done. Yeah, I could wax poetic about the stupidity of people on cellphones. And then, of course, I turn out to be just as bad.

Although   perhaps   with   much   better consequences . . .

I blame it all on Aunt Michelle, of course. She called just as I was sitting at the stoplight waiting to turn into the mall parking lot. And that woman can talk. With her the gift of the gab isn't a gift; it's a holy calling. But she makes it interesting, and I was still only halfway through an update on Uncle Joe's latest boating disaster by the time I'd parked.

At least I had an earpiece, but still I walked into the department store and paused just inside the entryway, forgetting why I was there.

'. . . and *then* the bucket of fish fell over. Slopped all over the ever-lovin' deck and just soaked my pants.'

I grinned silently at Aunty Mish's plight.

Jeans. I was here for jeans because Stan had accidentally washed two of the last three functional pairs I owned in hot water. With a red shirt. Sometimes I wondered if it was too much to ask for a lover with at least some modicum of common sense.

Stan's ability to quote John Donne in bed and expound on the Realists at length was charming. But when faced with the condition of my poor, unwillingly tie-dyed jeans, the Realists paled. Not to mention the fact that I loathe clothes shopping. Offhand, I could have thought of probably ten other things I would rather have spent my hard-won Friday morning off from work doing. But here I was.

'... Anyway. At least he'd had the life jacket on. Honestly, I think your uncle is the dumbest man alive sometimes.'

'I feel your pain, Aunty Mish. Believe me, I feel your pain.'

The door behind me opened and I stepped out of the way to let a woman with two teenagers and a noisy family of various and sundry ages pass. I really needed to just hurry up and get this over with; I could always call Aunty Mish back later. Or not. I was more than capable of multitasking, but either way I couldn't stand in the store entrance all day. And the last, littlest various and sundry was holding the inner door open by sheer willpower, and looking over his shoulder at me with a 'hurry up, lady!' expression.

Stifling a sigh so Aunty Mish wouldn't hear, I followed the other shoppers into the store and over to the rows of garish orange plastic carts. I probably didn't need one, but what the hell. OK, shopping cart: check. Women's clothing: to the left.

I've never bothered with the sections in clothing stores. They mean exactly squat to me. What the heck is a 'Misses' anyway? If I can find a pair of pants that fit, I simply consider it a miracle and thank the great deities of retail. So with my sights set on the distant racks of denim, I wheeled the cart around and started off.

Ah ha! There was a sale tag. Perfect. I stopped and continued to make agreeing murmurs to Aunty Mish as I dug patiently through the tangle of hangers and size tags. I swear, why the clothing industry thinks all women come in the same five or six sizes is beyond me.

'So how's that boyfriend of yours?'

'What?'

I wriggled a hanger free and considered the jeans on it. Beaded spangles on the pocket, but I supposed I could live with a few sparkles. Every piece of female apparel I looked at seemed to have been made for the teenage pop-star crowd, regardless of the section.

'Your boyfriend,' repeated Aunty Mish patiently. 'I never remember his name. But then, you never talk about him.'

'Oh. I . . .' I didn't know what to say. What could I say about Stan?

I racked my brains, trying to think of something suitably positive and affectionate. But standing there, faced with the choice of silver grommets or turquoise beads to adorn my backside, I wasn't feeling particularly generous towards Stanley. Deciding on the grommets as the lesser humiliation, I flung the pair into the cart and confessed to my aunt.

'It's Stan. And honestly, he's a pain in the ass more often than not. But he's decent in bed and he's smart. I guess that's about all there is to it.'

'That's all there is to it?'

I rifled through another row of hangers. 'Yes. What else should there be?'

'What do you think?'

She had me there. What else should there be?

We did all the right things. Books. Art. Candlelight on water. Long conversations. But I knew it was just going through the motions, and if I tried to argue the case to Aunty Mish she would see through it in a heartbeat.

I sighed, loud and audible this time. 'OK, OK, you win, but no lectures, darling. I'm happy enough.'

There was a pause while she thought it over. 'OK. No lecture. But ... you should be more than happy, Frannie. You should be ecstatic. Life's too short. Got it?'

Yeah, tell me something I didn't already know. 'Got it, Aunty M. Now talk about something else, please.'

She obliged, rambling off about my brother's baby's newest two teeth while I turned to search for a dressing room. And found it blocked for repairs. My luck I would come shopping in the middle of renovations.

'... but I can't figure out how to open this picture attachment.'

It was a plea for help. Great.

Luckily Aunty Mish isn't a total computer illiterate, but I still didn't want to do tech support in the middle of the lingerie section. I started walking while I tried to talk her through the download of Charles Jr's pictures, still looking for a dressing room. And found it, tucked behind rows of khakis. At least I think they were khakis, because Aunty Mish had lost herself in the complexities of .abm files versus

JPEGs and I was having a hell of a time trying to extricate her.

But once I felt sure she wasn't going to delete half her registry trying to save five baby pictures, I took my spangly selections from the cart and headed into the dressing room. I had no trouble finding a vacant stall without too many failed try-ons piled on the floor; I was the only one in the place.

I bolted the door and kicked off my sneakers. Then I stripped off my sweatpants, hung them over the stall partition as I bid goodbye to Aunty Mish, promised to call her later and turned off the earpiece. I reached for the first pair of jeans. And that's when the stall door next to me banged shut and I looked down to see a pair of decidedly male feet in sandals next door.

My first thought was to yell in a loud and unfriendly voice that he was in the wrong room. Until my gaze fell on the discarded clothes lying in my own stall. Dockers khakis, 32W, 34L. Ralph Lauren polo shirts. John Ashford sweater, XL.

Crap.

He had to have overheard me talking to Aunty Mish and if I could see his feet, he damn well could see mine, French manicured toes and all. His own feet were worth a second look. Smooth, well-kept nails, nicely defined ankles and just hairy enough to be sexy male without being caveman. I found myself imagining what the rest of those legs looked like. Amazing what not being on the phone can do for one's powers of observation.

I knew I should just play this off and act casual. Or put my pants on and get the hell out. But I did neither, simply stood there with my face burning, ogling the feet of a complete stranger as he undressed. Which he did without the least compunction. His shorts pooled around his ankles before he whisked them up, and then I jumped as they flopped halfway over the top of the partition.

'Sorry. Didn't mean to startle you. You can go ahead you know. I don't mind really.'

I could hear the laughter in his voice. And he was pulling on jeans, one leg at a time. Rustle. Zipper. I took a deep, deep breath and tried not to squeak when I spoke.

'Uh, thanks. I guess I should be the one apologising.'

A laugh. A deep, masculine laugh. 'Not at all. Mistakes happen.'

I fumbled with the clasps on the hanger and managed to get the jeans off after three tries. My fingers had apparently turned into blocks of wood at some point, or at least that's what they felt like. I got both legs in and pulled the pants up. Only at that point did I realise he now knew for a fact I'd been in my underwear. And would be again when I took these off. Never in my life have I been more tempted to shoplift. Just walk out of there and worry about paying for the jeans at the counter. Or not. Because he might walk out and see me. This would have been hysterical really ... had it been anyone but me.

'So do they fit?'

'I ... er ... what?'

'Do they fit? My sisters spend hours obsessing about finding pants that fit right. I think I've clocked them at three hours just on buying jeans before. But then...'

Zipper. One leg off, then another.

Boxers or briefs? I wondered.

'. . . they're fifteen and seventeen. So it figures.'

'Yeah, well, trust me, it gets harder with age,' I replied drily. I looked at my reflection. Surprisingly enough, these fitted, and the silver grommets didn't look half bad. I hadn't noticed it before, but a tiny silver horseshoe dangled from the belt loop over one hip. I jingled it and tried to decide if I had the metaphorical balls to take them off with him still there.

He was trying another pair on now, and in no great hurry apparently.

'But once you find a nicely fitting pair, it's worth it. From my perspective anyway.' He laughed again, teasing, and I found myself smiling in response. Never mind that he couldn't see.

'Oh really?' I jingled my horseshoe again, not really believing that I was striking up a flirtation in this situation. Yeah, I'd lost my mind for sure.

'Absolutely. I'll admit it; I'm a guy. I have the utmost appreciation for the loveliness of the female form. In denim, in khaki, in silk. You name it.'

Now I laughed out loud. 'Lovely, huh? Well, I certainly hope I can live up to that description.'

He paused. 'I'd offer to come around and give you an opinion, but I wouldn't want you to think I'm a total asshole.'

I leaned on the mirror and crossed one ankle over the other. Might as well be comfortable if I was going to have a full-blown conversation, right? 'I haven't gotten that impression so far. But I don't think I have the nerve to ask you for an opinion either.'

Another pause. I could tell he was still facing the mirror. I imagined him standing there, hands on hips, wondering what to say next.

'Can I offer one anyway? And you not throw something at me?'

'Offer away.' Why was my heart beating so fast? I waited.

'Well, I don't have a foot fetish or anything, but if your toes match the rest of you, I think lovely more than describes it.'

I covered my mouth with my hand and stared at the ceiling, laughing silently in disbelief. I felt like I'd been drinking champagne. Suddenly I didn't care about proper any more. 'I think that's the sexiest thing anyone's ever said to me.'

When he laughed, I heard the edge of nervous relief and I almost walked out of the stall then and there and knocked on his door. He'd been worried about *my* reaction. Simply insane! 'Well, you're most welcome.'

Zipper. Rustle. He was taking the second pair off. And then I decided, what the hell. What had Aunt Mish just said? Life's too short. Might as well make it interesting.

I waited until he had pulled them completely off before I asked, 'So, boxers or briefs?'

Silence. And then he laughed. 'Gentlemen don't tell.'

'There. Now I'm disappointed.'

I pushed away from the mirror and started to take the jeans off. My own underwear was starting to get decidedly damp. God, I couldn't believe I was getting worked up flirting with an unseen guy in a bloody dressing room. I didn't even have the excuse of being desperate. I had Stan. And hard on the heels of that thought was the realisation that I didn't want to think about Stan. Not right now.

'Oh, don't be disappointed. Give me a chance to critique the fit of those jeans over dinner and maybe I'll tell.'

Oh, he was smooth.

'Promise?' I asked.

'I said "maybe".'

'You don't make it easy do you?'

He started laughing. 'At the risk of sounding lame, no. I try to make it as hard as possible.'

I sat down on the narrow shelf under the mirror, and laughed until the tears ran down my face and my stomach hurt. Finally, when our laughter had subsided to chuckles, I looked down and saw that he had come to stand in the corner closest to where I sat.

'OK,' I said between gasps for breath. 'Dinner.'

'Great! Where would you like to meet?'

We haggled over a few places and finally agreed on a sushi restaurant across from the mall.

'At six?'

'Six is perfect.' I shook out the jeans I'd been holding, and waved them under the partition so he could see the horseshoe. 'I'll be wearing these and a pink sweater.'

I knew he was taking in every detail. I could almost see him nodding. 'Duly noted. I'll be waiting next to the aquarium and wearing sandals.' A pause and a little laugh. 'Wow! The only woman in the world who knows instantly what she's wearing to a date.'

I stood up and turned to the partition, my toes

facing his. 'I don't like to waste time making up my mind.'

'I can tell.' It was a compliment. 'You're definitely unique.'

'No, actually I'm Francesca, a.k.a. Frannie, a.k.a. various other less flattering things.'

A laugh. 'I'll stick with Francesca. I'm Cal.'

'Nice to, umm, meet you, Cal. Although I'm not sure meet is the word.'

'Me neither, but it works as well as anything.' He sighed. 'Right. Now I have to go figure out what *I'm* wearing tonight.'

I giggled. He was teasing again. Stan never teased.

He stepped away and I saw him pulling on his shorts, buckling his sandals. His arms and hands were like his feet. Dark hair. Definition even though there was no real muscle. Long fingers. No-nonsense hands.

Damn. If just those parts of him had this effect on my panties, what would seeing the rest of him do?

I pulled my sweats down from the partition as he opened the stall door and stepped out. He paused for just a moment outside my stall and through the wooden slats I could just make out a tall lean body. A runner's build. Holy Hot Mystery Men Batman.

'See you at six,' he said.

'I'll be there. Jeans and all and fully dressed, I promise.'

'Bye, Francesca.'

And with a laugh, he was gone. I stood there, clutching my sweats and grinning and wondering just what the hell I'd gotten myself into.

* * *

'I have a date.' I stuck my head around the down-stairs bathroom door and peered into the living room. He was reading with the TV on. 'With a guy I met in the dressing room.'

'Uh-huh.'

I waited but nothing more was forthcoming. With a sigh, I double-checked my get-up for the last time, turned off the bathroom light and walked into the living room.

'You don't believe me.'

Stan looked up from the book for all of the five seconds it took to roll his eyes at me.

I shrugged. 'Don't say I didn't tell you.'

He waved at me, never looking up. 'Have a good time. You look pretty.'

And that was all.

I'd been honest, I told my conscience. Yes, the truth was so outlandish it seemed nonsense. But something in my voice, in my face, in my posture would have given it away. If he had bothered to look.

But he hadn't and, thinking about it, I don't know that Stan had ever bothered to look that closely. I don't think he ever figured it necessary. And that was why I left the house and headed once again for the mall complex without a trace of regret.

As promised, he was waiting. Leaning against the wall beside the aquarium and watching a self-important goldfish make its way through the pillars of the plastic sunken castle. I stopped and I watched him, drinking in that scene and committing it to memory forever. Watching him just as the hostess was watching. And the two women to my right. And the teenage girl holding her boyfriend's hand and trying to appear not interested.

But when he looked up, his gaze found only me. I knew then what the favourites of the Bourbon kings must have felt like, being singled out by the one look that told me I was desired and chosen above all others. And I felt the envy of every other woman in that restaurant lobby as I walked, like one bewitched, to his side and smiled up at him.

He smiled back, and those eyes. Those eyes the colour of bottle-green glass polished smooth by the sea. I was bewitched, helpless to do anything but gaze at him as he bent down to brush his lips ever so modestly against my cheek and rest his hands, only for a burning, delicious moment, against my hips.

'I'm so glad you decided to come.'

'You thought I wouldn't?'

He nodded, full lips curving in a self-conscious smile. 'I thought you might decide it was just too crazy after all.'

'Crazy has never been a deterrent for me I'm afraid.'

I couldn't help it, I had to touch him. I reached up and brushed my fingers along the stubble of his jaw. One of those five-o'clock-shadow boys, no matter how often he shaved. I wanted to feel those rough cheeks brushing the insides of my thighs. I wanted those lips moving in slow kisses all over my body. I wanted that dark spiky hair dripping sweat as he lay over me, his hands braced above my head so he wouldn't brain me against the wall with every rough, hungry thrust.

So this was lust. And this was passion. And crazy

had never stopped me before. He blushed like a boy, something I'd never expected from my confident, dressing-room suitor. But his voice was as powerful and beguiling as ever.

'Don't look at me that way. I'm being tempted to suggest we just skip dinner totally.'

'Fine with me. I want an answer to my question, remember?'

He threw his head back and laughed, and slid an arm around my waist. 'Just for that, we'll have dinner and go to a movie *and* go for a walk. And *then*...' He pressed one finger to the tip of my nose. 'I'll take you home and kiss you goodnight right there. And that's all you'll get, missy.'

I stuck my tongue out at him and we walked to the hostess's podium giggling like schoolgirls, his arm still curled comfortably around my waist. Holy Mother of heaven. If I didn't know better, I'd have thought I was falling in love.

I knocked the phone off the dresser in my hurry to answer it, dived after it and then sat on the floor to talk. Grinning as I answered.

'Meet me?'

Damn, I loved the sound of his voice. 'Where?' I asked.

'I don't know. For coffee? I don't care; I just want to see you. And I picked last time.'

I tried to remember if he *had* picked last time, but I'd lost track. Was this the fifth date or the sixth? I was still racking my brains when he gave an impatient sigh fifteen seconds later.

'You know what? Screw that. Meet me at the mall

and come back to my place and I'll make you breakfast.'

'Breakfast? It's three o'clock.'

'Right. You come over this afternoon; I'll make you breakfast in the morning.'

I was speechless. Here it was. I'd longed for it, thought about it constantly, fantasised about it and dreamed of him asking me. And now I had no idea what to say. 'And what do I tell Stan?' I wondered aloud.

'Tell him you're coming over to fuck me silly. It's not like he'll listen anyway.'

I sighed. Cal was probably right. After the first night, I'd simply told Stan I was going out, going shopping. Never mind that every time I came home empty-handed. He barely looked up.

I think Stan knew; I think he cared even less.

'Meet you in an hour,' I said.

We met at the ice-cream counter and then walked from store to store for an hour, sharing a cone. Tangling our tongues with each lick. Hands in each other's back pockets like a couple of starry-eyed youngsters dropped off at the mall to buy hassled parents a few peaceful hours. We didn't care. Half-way through life isn't too late to fall.

When we finally got sick of the ice cream and dumped it in a convenient trash can, we found ourselves before the mall entrance of The Store. Our store. Other people had special songs, special restaurants and cities. We had the men's dressing room at a department store. I wouldn't have traded it for the most romantic boulevard in Paris.

'Want to visit old haunts?' he asked with a mischievous smile.

'I'm game if you are.'

And so we wandered in without apparent hurry. Through rows of polyester cotton, denim and lace, and soft wool blends, until at last we found ourselves in the dressing room once again. Most of the stalls were partitioned off with yellow tape and construction notices, and a makeshift wall obscured the front entrance, forcing us to go around it. We did, and found ourselves alone except for a crowd of dust flakes whirling in the air, which smelled of plaster and raw wood.

Cal turned and slid his hands under my sweater. Hands warm and slightly damp on my bare waist, he pulled me close. His mouth was mint-chocolate-chip sweet from the ice cream; his tongue hot and impatient. He licked the corners of my mouth and purred in appreciation.

'You taste good.'

I giggled nervously. Wasn't this what I'd been hoping for?

But it's a really, really bad idea chimed the voice of reason. Bad, stupid, utterly humiliating, criminal-record kind of bad.

'We can't do this here.'

'Can't we?' His hands slid further up my torso; his fingertips pressed against the underwire of my bra. 'Tell me, Frannie, if you'd seen me before the dressing room, wouldn't you have fucked me that day?'

'No,' I whispered. But his fingers were under the wire and the satin and I wasn't so sure any more.

Suddenly he pulled away and looked over my

head. He frowned a moment and then smiled. 'Come on.'

'What? Wh...?' But he was already heading for the first aisle of stalls and down to the very last one on the row.

'Here.'

He pushed open the door and pulled me in, then bolted it behind. The room was big enough for both of us but he blocked me from taking so much as a single step away from the closed door. Hands on the wall to either side of the slats, he kissed me again, hips rubbing mine. And I felt the warm heavy bulge pressing through his jeans into my stomach. His need; like mine. Hot. Urgent.

'I want you to undress for me. In front of the mirror.' His teeth tugged at my lower lip. 'Tease me.'

Tease. That I could do. I hooked my hands into the waist of his pants, pulling him closer, grinding that lovely hardness into me.

'Then will I get an answer to my question?' I asked, laughing.

He frowned for a minute, and then smiled as he remembered, but he was short of breath already and growing more so. 'You'll get anything you want.'

'Fair enough.'

I squeezed past and spun around, looking at him from the other side of the room. Christ on a bike, the man was hot. He leant half on the door, half on the frame and lifted a finger, twirled it like he was stirring a drink.

'Face the mirror.'

I made a face, but obeyed. And then hesitated. This was so not the thing to do, and two months ago would have been all but unthinkable. But now I had Cal, standing behind me with his gorgeous, naughty smile and his hard-on, and so now ... now I didn't care.

I reached for the zipper of my sweatshirt and tugged it down half an inch. Black satin bra and the shadow of cleavage. I looked up and found his gaze in the mirror; he smiled approval. Another half-inch; another pause. And then I dragged it all the way down until the zipper pulled apart entirely and I could shake the sweatshirt off. I saw him move, saw his hand stray to his groin. Still smiling.

One bra strap; another. Then the hooks, and the bra joined the sweater. I reached for the buttons on my pants and only then remembered I was wearing The Jeans, silver horseshoe and all. He, of course, had noticed from the start. He always noticed. Well, I'd leave them on. For now.

Instead I turned my attention to my naked breasts, the nipples already tight with excitement. I pinched them hard and felt the pleasure swell between my legs. Harder. I bit my lip and looked up at Cal. The lazy casual smile was gone. I said his name once, not loud, barely more than a whisper.

But he came to me.

He crossed the dressing room in a single long-legged stride to stand behind me and curve his hands over my upper arms. His lips touched my neck, soft, while the rough promise of beard on his chin and cheeks grazed my bare skin. It sent chills through me – that kiss, raising the hair on my neck and my arms, making the muscles of my stomach clench. His hands took mine away from my chest, brought them behind me.

'Touch me.' It was a low growl and still a plea. But he didn't even have to ask. I wanted to touch him, kiss him, do everything I could think of with my mouth and my hands and my body to him.

Easier said than done. I fumbled with buttons, trying to think past his cashmere-sandpaper kisses on my neck and his pinching, kneading, stroking hands on my naked tits. For a frustrated moment I wondered how women in historical romance novels ever managed their forbidden jollies dealing with cravats and waistcoats when I couldn't even get a fucking pair of jeans off a man. But at last my efforts were rewarded.

And it figures, it was boxer briefs after all. Smiling, I wriggled my fingers through denim and one hundred per cent cotton and found his cock. Though heaven knows it wasn't hard to find at all. I could just barely get my thumb and middle finger wrapped around it. Sweet Jesus, I'd never even known they came in this size. I pulled it out and began to stroke him up and down, rubbing the tip against the skin of my back, and he moaned. His hands closed hard on my breast and my stomach and he went still.

'God, Frannie.'

As I stroked down, I let my touch keep going, let my fingers run light and tickling over his balls still tucked safely into his briefs, and I won a short involuntary thrust against my back.

'Like that?' I asked.

Only a sigh for an answer. His eyes were closed.

I ran one hand back up his cock, reaching around to squeeze his ass closer with the other. At the tip I could get my fingers closed around him, and I jacked him off until I felt a tiny spurt of pre-come, wet and warm on my back. And answering wet delicious warmth in my own jeans.

His hands were sliding down my front now, opening my jeans, tugging them down. I let go of him to help, pushing the material down to my knees, but when he reached for my panties I stopped him. I found his reflected gaze, his eyebrows lifted in a silent question.

'No need for that.'

I bent forwards so that my ass and my pussy were raised to his view, and braced one palm on the mirror. I'd bought these panties just for him. For today. I hadn't lied *every* time I told Stan I was going shopping; every now and then I'd come home with a few special purchases.

Now I pulled the folds of lace apart over the seamless crotch and teased my bare slit with one finger, half-breaking my neck in the process just to see his reaction in the mirror. His expression was all I'd hoped for. And then we heard the rustle of fabric, footsteps, movement. We stopped breathing. A stall door banged somewhere towards the front of the dressing room.

Grinning, I began rubbing my finger against my clit harder, rubbing it in circles and figures of eight as I got wetter and wetter, and Cal's face blushed redder and redder. He shook his head at me, mouthing at me to stop. But I ignored him. Hadn't he asked to be teased?

From the distant stall, came the sound of clothing being removed. Poor guy had no idea what he was missing just a few walls away. I slid a finger into my pussy, then another. I bent my head and arched my back down. I'd lose the pleasure of seeing Cal's tormented desire, but I knew the effect I was having. I wriggled my fingers deeper, then began sliding my hips back and forth, moving my hand in counter thrust; shivering as the air of the dressing room touched my flushed, perspiring skin.

And then I almost jumped. Hot hard flesh pressed against my ass; a strong male hand gripped it. He slid his cock across my soaked lace panties, pushing it into the yielding softness beneath. My fingers got out of the way. And then ... then I thought I must scream or burst as the head of his cock squeezed into my super-aroused pussy. And that was just the tip. Oh God.

I flung my other hand out for support against the wall beside the mirror and winced at the slap it made. But I couldn't judge if the noise was loud enough to be heard. The blood was rushing to my head and Cal was thrusting into me with slow strokes, going deeper every time. And I couldn't think at all. I bit my lip and ground myself against him, loving the bursts of pleasure every time I pressed an extra-sensitive spot. Not caring about anything but Cal inside of me.

A stall door banged far, far away. It meant nothing to me, lost in pleasureland, until Cal's hands on my waist pulled me upwards. He slid out and I squeaked in disappointment, but his fingers covered my lips as he spun me around. He knelt and dragged my boots off, my jeans. And then as he rose, he lifted my thighs.

I tried to help, bracing my feet on the shelf under the mirror, and almost fell, clumsy with desire and distraction. But he laughed softly and held me, worked himself back into me. And then, with the cold mirror on my back and my arms around his neck. With him kissing me hard to stifle my moans of pleasure because his magnificent cock was sending my pussy and my clit wild with satisfaction. And because all the rest of him was sending everything else in me wild with happiness.

There, in that dressing room as I came and came and came all over his cock. As I heard him grunt and sigh, and felt come running hot down my legs. Then I knew what it was like to really and truly make love.

'You still owe me breakfast,' I said, once we'd safely made it out unnoticed and were casually strolling among rows of socks as if nothing at all unusual had happened in the last hour. As if we hadn't just committed a Class-A misdemeanor.

'Are you coming home with me?' he asked, arm about my waist, fingers tucked intimately under the hem of my sweatshirt. I sniffed him. Sweet musky smell of cologne and sex and faint laundry detergent on his clothes. I cuddled closer. Why was I even still haggling over the decision?

He leant down and whispered in my ear. 'Hurry up and decide. My underwear's all soggy.' He paused, then added in an aggrieved tone, 'Which is *your* fault by the way.'

I laughed. 'Quit being such a fusspot.' I turned down an aisle and grabbed a packet of cotton boxer-briefs from the shelf. Large. 'Here.'

He looked down and smiled. 'I see you were paying attention after all.'

He looked up and I couldn't find anything to say. Not with those eyes looking at me like that.

Life's too short.

'On second thought, put them back,' I said. 'You won't need any once I get you home.'

He grinned. The package fell to the floor and I was being kissed. Really kissed. And I was ecstatic.

Aunty Mish would be glad. And Stan? Well, he'd complain for appearance's sake at first. And, of course, he'd complain to everyone else about me too, but then it would be over and he'd go back to his books and his pontificating. And God help his next girlfriend and her laundry.

On the way to the parking lot I dug that troublemaking cellphone out of my pocket with the hand not holding Cal's and called Aunty Mish to tell her I'd gone shopping and found a perfect fit.

A. D. R. Forte has had several short stories published in themed Wicked Words anthologies.